CHIEFS

Michael Trammell

Hysterical Books
2026

Chiefs by Michael Trammell — First Edition

Cover Image, Design, production: Jay Snodgrass

LOC: 2026936460
ISBN — 978-0-940821-39-2

Hysterical Books is dedicated
to the publication and appreciation of fine poetry
and other literary genres.

HYSTERICAL BOOKS
1506 Wekewa Nene
Tallahassee Florida

Published in the United States by Hysterical Books
Tallahassee, Florida • First Edition, 2026
hystericalbooks.com
hystericalbooks@gmail.com

With much love always . . .
this book is for Ariel, Dylan,
and Mary Jane

Acknowledgements

Thanks to my mother for encouraging my love for language.

Thanks to my brother, Barry, for his creative spirit and insights.

Thanks to my late father for always gently pushing me towards the next goal.

And a big thanks to all writers and teachers in the communities I've been fortunate enough to be a part of, especially the members of the MIR Station / 4th Quarter / Wings crew over the past 30+ years, including R. Gamero, T. Welch, J. Reynolds, C. Miranda, L. Kitchen, R. Franklin, C. Hayes, P. Laffan, R. Wiginton, M. Gearhart, G. Clark, T. McWhirter, D. Newman, M. McClelland, J. Clark, N. Stuckey-French, V. Suarez, P. Busby, T. Schneider, M. Rychlik, P. MacEnulty, R. Smith, M. Canter, M. Hobson, and J. Needle.

Grateful acknowledgement is made to the *Sandhill Review* in which the following chapters/poems appeared: "Old Crow at the Indian Mound at Night" and "Attan and the Green Corn Dance."

Time is more fundamental than space.
It is, indeed, the most pervasive
of all the categories
in other words
theres plenty of it.
and it stretches things themselves
until they blend into one,
so if youve seen one thing
youve seen them all.

--Edward Dorn, *Gunslinger*

"For it's my opinion, begging your worship's pardon, that it was all fraud
and fictions, or at least that you dreamt it."
"Everything is possible."

--Miguel de Cervantes, *Don Quixote*

Fragments from the poem "How to Write the Great American Indian Novel":

All of the Indians must have tragic features: tragic noses, eyes, and arms....
Indians always have secrets, which are carefully and slowly revealed.
Yet Indian secrets can be disclosed suddenly, like a storm.
Indian men, of course, are storms....
Alcohol should be consumed. Cars must be driven at high speeds.
Indians must see visions....
                              White people must carry
an Indian deep inside themselves. Those interior Indians are half-breed
and obviously from horse cultures....
                              Sometimes there are complications....
There must be redemption, of course, and sins must be forgiven.
For this, we need children....
In the Great American Indian novel, when it is finally written,
  all of the white people will be Indians
  and all of the Indians will be ghosts.

--Sherman Alexie

How I Met Old Crow

*--My initial encounter with Old Crow of the Calusa tribe and
subsequent Adventures at sea on the Santa María.*

The Calusa still live in the Everglades
of southwest Florida, or did, and there
I met a man who'd lead his tribe, or might
if they returned,
the unacknowledged possible great, great
grandnephew of Chief Osceola,
he claimed, nicknamed
John Jumper or Cowkeeper
or Billy-Panther, depending on weather,
but named at birth Ochafanwaw,
Native American blackbird king—
An Indian Chief! a phrase that made
him laugh. He worked on

the *Niña*, the *Pinta*, and the *Santa
María* as a Spanish first mate for reenactments
of the Columbus kind. Onboard (*and always?*)
he kept a tobacco plug inside his cheek
(or it seemed a colossal gumball?) that I later
learned was more than chaw
and fueled a world.

He claimed it good as any job,
and talked it up in a Fort Myers joint,
grew garrulous while we chatted
by happenstance at the waterside
Cabbage Key Bar; faded dollar
bills stapled to the ceiling, clouds
of beige and green. I'd been fired

from a warehouse job on the gulf
that seemed too fishy
and I sat at a point in stasis,
a barstool, my pockets stoked
with severance pay, so I bought
the Old Crow a Crown Royal.
An hour in, he'd talked
me into joining his crew;
all I had to do
was *lift* my weight in rope
and cargo. Or gold. And at that,
he laughed. The Calusa had always
shooed the Spanish up the coast
by insisting the Apalachee
had bling steeped in steepheads
valleyed between red clay hills.

Was he Queequeg? (or maybe Ahab?)
as he had me climb aboard
the Santa María, I a poor man's
Ishmael lost in a Spanish *Pequod*,
the Pequod a New England tribe
called *Pequot* by the Algonquins
because they knew, just as Calusa too,
they were *men of the swamp*.

Our three ships went sailing out
on Christmas Day, or so it felt
because the job was a gift and
Virgin Mary swam above water
and below my feet, and so I surfed
upon her holy back. And at noon,
instead of prayer, Old Crow

whipped out a sacred Scepter, *no,*
Innuit harpoon, *no,* a dart or spear,
still no, just a mostly sanded
tree-branch stick bent and carved
for mysterious purpose. Or not.
He leisurely scratched his backside
as he one-handedly climbed
to crow's nest with his viewing glass
a-strap his neck and chewed his chaw.

With a pointed finger he had me swabbing
decks with holystone, the pumice pummeling
fungus from the boards. I knelt as if praying
to scrape the stone across the wood
with a mix of sea and sand
to make the deck whiter than my hand.

Old Crow pointed with his lips
to one board or two. He chanted
softly to the gulls that hovered near
his nest and eyed his idle stick
poking from a pocket. His voice
sliced along the lapping waves
and cut the trough deeper
between the swells.

We head north. Clay makes mountains
there. We have wins to take,
and this wind will push us
till we make St. Marks
and dock beside where rivers meet.

I wished the wind to whip us,
let us land lashed and wet
but done, so that my knees
could lift from wood and I'd
be paid and allowed to leave.

That night my gut roiled,
but Crow made me eat bland mullet
in a strange gruel designed to quell
the stomach. I settled and slept, but
Ochafanwaw circled the deck
with eyes as large as Scrawled Cowfish
ojos, each beneath spiney horns
as if fish-gods of the carapace-kind.

Dawn sun on stern. Old Crow shook me,
muttering, whispered names like rolling dice
to see which one might win. I raised a lid,
and he began to stutter. He called himself
John Jumper, next *Cowkeeper*, then
Billy-Panther. Talked of nightmare,
of manta rays and cockle shells and dark days
past. Then paused. He asked *Do you know
Joe Yaqui or John Hawk or Navajo Joe?
You knew them in my dreams. You
were barrelman of the foremast
and could point the way.*

But I didn't know them.

They are the same man, Crow said.
*You know him. As Quint Asper too.
The Bandit. Paul Crewe.*

I squinted as sun stung my face.
Burt Reynolds? The Longest Yard? Who,
50+ years ago, played tailback at FSU?
The movie star?

Crow said, *We must find him.*

I replied, *He's dead.*

Not true. And in the dreams you knew,
he's half-Cherokee too. In hiding
at the Mission. You knew his mound
is not grave but home. And you stood true.

Sir Reál (of Spain)

   --A meditation on the protean nature of time and space.

Where and when are we?
In a time not real or surreal?
A space or a place where a royal

conquistador, the Sir-Real (of Spain),
can balance a globe on the tip of
a hummingbird's wing?

The present, the past, the never now
all have a claim to this.

And we are now in it.

Johari Window

*   --A dream about the past concerning a lecture on concepts
mostly abstract and slippery.*

Aboard ship that night
I dreamt of the days
I'd taught college kids
in Central Florida
content that I sometimes
sensed I misunderstood
or doubted was useful.
In the dream, the classroom
was aboard the ship,
and Old Crow was my latest
pupil. We discussed
the Johari Window theory
of communication, a way for
one to understand another,
especially if a large gulf existed
between the two. In the vision-
scape a four-paned window engulfed
the stern, one large square labeled
the *Unknown.* The word *Johari,*
at that moment in the dream,
neither of us knew,
as it sounded like a tribe,
such as Yaqui,
but had no referent as such. Yet
it meant *Flower of the Desert*
in Swahili and *Jewel* in
Arabic and a dialect of Kumaoni,
in of all places,
India.

The window had four stained panes;
each glass square bared
a see-through label: *Blind-
spot, Arena, Façade, Unknown.*
I was professor but drew a blank.
Could these four words make us
aware of our biases?

Crow looked up from his textbook
and smiled; *Do you know where
they got the name Johari?* he asked.
Their own names, Joe and Harry.
Crow laughed and laughed
and couldn't stop.

Landfall

*--How Old Crow and I disembarked at St. Marks, met Antonia
of Cuba, traveled to Tallahassee, and jumpstarted a fierce rivalry
with Chief Buffalo of the Miccosukee.*

The three Spanish caravels
sailed through the shallow
inlet and passed the sawgrass
of the lighthouse levee
to dock near dead
quiet Fort San Marcos
de Apalache. Old Crow
helped set the ships
for visitors. I tied ropes
and hoped to quit. Holy-
stoning had broke
my back and knees.

But Crow had a shipless
job in mind for me
to block and tackle
and pull myself to shape.
He needed a caddy,
of sorts, to help him
with a ballgame.

This week was well-earned
shore leave, and Crow had
aligned his dates with harvest
moon that fully lit the sky,
another ball of sorts. So he
had tee times neatly cupped
within his days it seemed.

Foolishly, I said *yes*. Yes, I needed
work to pad an empty savings.
I lacked the cash to pay cell phone
bills, though all the calls to home
I'd not yet made. Yes, it's true,
I'd stopped calling.

We jumped ship. But not before
collecting tickets from one round
of tourists. Crow helped aboard
a turista Cubana, grave of face
but broad of smile, she wore
a Counting Crows concert shirt
of July 4, 1997. He happily mirrored
her Cuban accent with his own
fake one. Her name was Antonia.
He enjoyed calling her Doña Antonia
and watching her smile grow brighter
than a necklace of polished cowrie shells.

I worked the reenactment side,
demonstrating how Columbus'
crew painstakingly unraveled
and reduced to fiber old tar-thick
ropes and cordage and then showed
how they'd plug ship's leaks
with these spongy scraps
mixed with pine sap, a patch-paste
called oakum. Antonia studied
my work with sincere aplomb,
but Crow soon beseeched her
to climb the foremast.

Antonia owned a Mustang. As
the tour ended, she offered a
ride to Tallahassee. Crow,
slipping from a Havana accent, noted
how in Muskogee-Creek
the word meant *Old Town*.
How old? she asked. Old Crow
grinned. *No older than famous
ballgames*. He winked and chopped
his arm as if launching a pig-
skin. She laughed, ignored
his accent change. I sighed.
It would be a long ride.

By some twisted luck,
we ended up at Saint Andrews,
a downtown pub serving nary
a pint but many a politico
handheld. A menu included sweet
Gov Graham Cracker S'more
for dessert. Antonia ordered

a DeSantis Fishy Sandwich
and I ordered a Coke. Crow
passed on the Fishermen's special
and requested a shellfish plate.
Raw oysters were his fave, as he
could slurp them past the ball
of chaw that filled his cheek.

And, by happenstance, this
being special session, Miccosukee
Chief *Buffalo* Tiger, Jr., also known
as Heenehatche Jr., was lobbying
for 2,000 more slots at the Casino
& Resort, and stumbled
against our table to rant
and rave at our friend *Ochafanwaw*
to pour more salt on a rift
that see-sawed in the nowhere
here and there of time not-time.

Yes, we sat in a restaurant,
so when I smelt a sweet draft
vaguely like bacon, I thought nothing
of it, as Crow sat silent and Buffalo
bellowed. Until I saw the wood sticking
straight from Buffalo's pocket:
it had the odor of hickory
and stank the same as what Crow
slyly slid from behind his back.

What to make of this violence
that interrupted the house
of a Saint? Spanish missionaries
at ol' Iglesia San Luis might have
wondered too.

Buffalo launched across the table—
my cola waterfalled to my lap,
then shoes; the ice rattling,
coughing—and wrapped
both his hands around Crow's
neck and squeezed as if
strangling a demon.
The patrons scrambled out
as if bursting from a pipe.

Erupting from Crow's
windpipe came not tobacco
but a ball of hair-
stuffed deerskin the size
of a killifish that he'd
once caught for bait.

Antonia held up a menu
like a shield, and the ball
bounced off, and Buffalo
caught it on the end
of his stick. He followed
the flood; Crow flew
after. I, Coke-soaked,
trailed Crow.

We'd gone from landfall
to waterfall to
stickball.

I held his hickory
branch. I fell
to my work.
From what

I knew,
he had
to win

this battle
this bet
this game.

Miccosukee

*   --Our tracking of Chief Buffalo to a nearby village, and how the
*dreaded Stikini kept him from scoring within the **universe** of the epic
stickball game.*

Is due northeast of Tallahassee
by 21 miles, fewer as the Crow
flies. The Miccosukee people were of
Creek origin, and soon became a branch
of the Seminole nation. Some 70
warriors patrolled the outskirts, this
capital of the short-lived State
of Muskogee. And riding
Antonia's Mustang, she and I
and Crow chased Buffalo
and his Bronco straight to
this village where a pole
marked a goal. Buffalo
had his stick atop the deerskin
ball in a bucket seat
and hauled ass towards
Moccasin Gap where the road
narrows under a canopy
of live oaks, sweet gums,
hickory, moss, and pines.

Crow had to block the shot,
blacken the dot, keep the other
from leaving a spot at the pole's
position below the dead magnolia
where the owl-witches, stoic Stikini,
defended with dreadful long talons,
sharpened-on-pop-ash claws. Or so
he hoped. Time had been a slow
drifter in his reckoning of the
stamina of these faithful but fateful
creatures. It had been a few winters.

The Stikini goalie sticks were thick
as midsized sabal palms, the cabbage kind
that thrive along the Apalachicola River.

    Mustang and Bronco come screeching and halt
    where Hwy 59 crosses 142. They find no brethren,
    and the Bronco then conks. Kaput!
    But for Crow and Buffalo, the game
    remains. Buffalo balances the ball at the end
    of the stick as if it were glued
    but it's not. Crow grabs his hickory branch
    from me, his caddy. First one, then the other plow
    into forest, bat at fronds to find their way to goal.

Two look-alike Stikini stood before the magnolia
and blocked all Buffalo could throw at them.
Their owl-beaks cackled with taunts and the near-
primate chants of barred owls. They threatened
to eat Buffalo's and Crow's hearts. Then Buffalo
blinked first and dashed from Miccosukee,
scrambling north by northwest.

Foshalee

*--Of the trailing of Buffalo through wilderness and of the former
whereabouts of the buckskin stickball.*

Is an Apalachee word
that means *dry water.*

Foshalee Lake and Slough
are wet. But sometimes dry.

Weather makes *the when.*
We followed Buffalo to water

but lost the trail. The trail
ran dry. Crow slowed.

Antonia and I caught
our breath at the banks

of Foshalee. Crow sat.
He stared at his stick.

Me: *You've had that
deerskin in your mouth*

for how long?
Crow: *Maybe years.*

Me: *And that guy
knew?* I shook my head.

Crow: *I suspect
he suspected. Once*

I too disappeared
into the forest.

He sighed, grimaced,
then smiled.

Yes, with the ball.
Antonia laughed.

She: *And you hid*
it in your mouth

like a stick of gum
I might have kept

on a bedpost
as a child?

Crow: *Since the last*
stickball gathering,

yes. The game was tied.
I'd been cursed,

could only miss. They were
too close to winning,

just needed one goal.
I'd placed too much

at stake. And I could not
afford to lose

my biggest bet of all.

Goalpost

--An explanation of the Native stickball game's goalpost.

Let's describe the pole.
What is it? A single goal-
post much taller than

a Christmas tree, but triangular,
flat, not so wide. More like
a holiday tree with a very long trunk.
At post's top,

snail shells at the edge,
a nest on the tiptop,
and in the nest,
a stuffed bald eagle.

One point when it hits
the goalpost, and two points if
it lands inside the eagle's nest.
First to eleven wins.

But did the game ever end?
Many times played from village
to village, pole to pole,
spanned by miles. All while

the Spanish sought
to ban the game
but couldn't. Too
violent, they decried,

if only it was a cross!

Buffalo is Lost

>   *--Crow's musings on Buffalo's next move.*

Crow, while laughing: *Don't*
matter where Buffalo go. The other
post has moved, and he'll never find it.

Not without help.

But for now, he holds
the game and ball
in the balance.

He may have gone to the gridiron
bowl, because folks say it's
The Home of the Seminoles.

West and South to the Football Bowl

>   *--Of my and Antonia's past, Burt Reynold's legacy, and a*
>   *camp-out atop a tall Indian Mound.*

We treaded slowly through wooded
corridors, meandering to the city's center,
leaving the Mustang where Antonia
parked it, and we took turns
unfolding tales to pass the time.

What had been our past
times, the near and distant
days that had led us to now
in these tall timbers?

I'd grown up east of Everglades,
east of Loxahatchee, in neighborhoods
of the New, as in York and Jersey folk,
and the stickball we'd played sported
a broom handle and a Spaldeen, the game
stretching from Miami to Boca
but originally spawned from Northern
city streets just south of New England.
Years that followed were marked
or marred by school and work
and school until I'd piled degrees that took
me into the high trees of academia: the title
of professor. But a year ago
I'd quit. Gone numb. Students, faculty,
admin had changed and I hadn't. And I
needed to get my nails dirty: warehouse
and fishboat jobs, things more hands-on,
more visceral, more real.

Antonia had grown up
in Cuba and studied at the Universidad
de la Habana. She'd managed to immigrate
to Florida via a web of interconnections,
her own schemata of sorts, but in Cuba
had started a dissertation on American Movie
Actors of the '70s as Anti-Capitalists.

And who's that? asked Crow, who'd been
quiet for near half an hour. He suddenly
handed me his hickory stick, and I knew
it was time for me to return as caddy.
Do you mean the Stars? he asked.
Sure, she answered. *Lee Grant of Shampoo.*

*Paul Newman, of course, too. Faye Dunaway
maybe. Even Burt Reynolds.*

Not true, I said.

Crow glared at me wide-eyed. *He is native.
He knows the land and its people.*

Knew, I said. I shook the stick at him.

It is possible, Antonia corrected. *Compare
Jean-Luc Goddard's Weekend with Smokey
and the Bandit II.*

The Bandit? I cried. *The sequel?* I sighed.
I was surrounded by slash pines, scrub oaks,
and madness.

They're both anti-consumerism, she said.

*I stand consumed by your critique
and spit-out to dry in words too big
to fail.* I fell silent, but whipped
the hickory back and forth as if
a conductor on a bender.

We walked in quiet for quite a while,
only the chittering of red-bellied
woodpeckers teased us.

Antonia cleared her throat.
She'd arrived here to help *su abuela,*
who'd left Cuba long ago. Her
parents were encamped in Venezuela

and couldn't wander, so she came
to the States as a caretaker. But
abuela passed away last year, and now
with an inheritance, Antonia was learning
a landscape she hadn't had a chance
to know. Bought a Mustang
and told herself, *Here I go!*

Are you still a communist? I asked.
She shrugged. *A communist in the land
of commerce? I am maybe neither
or both. And what about you? U.S.
universities are full of communists,
aren't they?*

I wouldn't know, I sighed. *I taught communications
in the Business School.*

Speaking of commerce, I continued, *Crow,
what exactly did you bet? I hope it wasn't
crypto-change or derivatives of synthetic
CDOs (quite illegal now, you know).
Was it cash or land or title?*

A way of life, perhaps, said Crow.

The scrabbling of a nearby wakeful
armadillo in the scrub palms clashed
with the distant roadside song of tires
on Highway 27. We were nearing
city limits. Crow glanced at both of us.
The day is late. We should bivouac

on dry ground at the Okeeheepkee
Lake Jackson Mounds. Spend the
night and await the dawn. I'll hunt,
fish, make fire and beds. We will
let the night carry us on.

Bivouac? I asked.

I joined the army for one year
and one day. Then I returned.
I choose to forget it now.

A barred owl hooted above us,
and a return song echoed from
densely-packed pines to our south.

We're close, Crow said.

We reached the tallest manmade hill
and climbed to the top. The sun set.
This mound has good bones, he sighed.
Wings cut the sky, swooping, drifting,
living arrows, the flights of Mississippi
and Swallowtail Kites. They made silent
circles. Old Crow did as he'd said,
sparking fire, weaving a lean-to from limbs
and vines, shaping beds of leaves
and pine straw. He cooked bass
he'd fished from the nearby lake,
and we ate. The stars appeared
and sang old songs, perhaps had been
humming them since today at Miccosukee,
the voices of the starlight beaming
streams of time for hours and hours,

making our journey through the county
seemingly set in a time sixty
or seventy years ago. I'd wondered why
we'd seen so few neighborhoods as Crow
led us through trees and sloughs
and steepheads; now I knew.

What did you teach at the college?
asked Antonia. *And where?*

Seminole County Tech. Small,
compact, affordable. Bravest students
from nearby Apopka. Some called them
dangerous, those tough South Apopka kids,
which is kind of funny since the word
in the Timucuan language means maybe
Big Potato or Tater Eating Place . . .
or Spud Chowing Folk.

Calusa knew the Timucua, Crow mumbled,
but then closed his eyes and leaned
towards the fire. I opened my throat.

I taught the business bull, the walk and the talk,
how to speak, what to wear, how to write,
the tech-squawk for the big bucks. Some kids
said Apopka is the most gangster town in Florida,
and I was teaching them big business for dealing
the finest drugs, because there's not a lot to do
in a town with a polluted lake, water choked
from Gourd Neck Spring by sewage and farmland
runoff. They called home APK, also "chopper city"—
the machine guns floating everywhere. One told me
that an Apopka Gentleman is a cocktail polluted

by Four Loko and two roofies.

This was Seminole County Technical College,
and I held my ground for ten years. It was
hardened ground. And I grew too hard
or not hard enough. Or all around me
grew stoney or muck-filled or both. I cared
deeply, and then something broke, and I
could no longer care. I resigned. The kids
called me the last gentleman at SCTC,
but, since I was abandoning them, I felt
a fraud and knew I deserved no applause.

Old Crow whispered to a raccoon at the edge
of the ring of firelight. The wind had died.
Smoke rose in a line to sky and stars. He nodded.

Antonia stirred. *Here I'm learning a Spanish heritage.*
That's my reward for becoming American. My
father's side served kings of Toledo and Madrid,
and now I trace the roots of those thrones
that spread here to Florida and beyond. I left
home, left Cuba, but now I'm finding my family
legacy locked into this misshapen peninsula.
Old castillos and dry wells and musty missions,
I search each to feel the past wed my bones.

Calusa knew the Spanish, Crow whispered,
but then sat up straighter and leaned
away from the fire. A tiny ember floated up
and vanished. The moon appeared.

I'm searching too, I said. Maybe for another
school? Some place where the fit feels
better? Or maybe I hunt for my own
lost soul. I don't know.

Crow lifted his head and searched the night sky.
When Breath Maker, Creator, Hisagita Misa,
molded the earth, he wanted so many things.
Birds, reptiles, insects, mammals. But of all,
his favorite was the patient Panther.

Coo-wah-chobee, crawls on four legs, close
to the ground. The Panther had waited quietly
inside the Creator's shell with the other beings,
and when the Wind split an opening,
the Panther first appeared, and Creator loved it.

But Panther was skittish and would not linger
near Creator who so longed
to stroke the long, soft hairs along the spine, so

he breathed a new spirit inside the feline,
and the cat was then a good companion.
With that, Breath Maker gave the Panther
the forest's truths for medicine
to heal all fevers and ailments
and memories.

Am I a cat? I asked.

Antonia laughed. *No, you need*
a new soul. A good one.

I glared at her and tapped the ball
stick at the fire's edge.

Crow then spun blankets from leaves
and vines and covered us gently.
The fire cooled but wind gusts
kept it blinking all night.

U. S. Army

   --Of Old Crow's time in the Army.

On that day a decade or longer past,
he stood onstage at *Seminole*

Hard Rock Hotel and Casino
as the tribe's only active-duty member

having served a tour in Afghanistan.
He'd returned last night. Through red

eyes he'd watched and listened as Seminole
colors were presented by the tribe's

Florida Color Guard, and The Red Boys
pow-wow singers performed The National Anthem.

The program had a special surprise: handshakes
from several members of the Florida Panthers,

his favorite sports team. The club promised to ship
team gear to his unit overseas. A former tribal

chief told him, *Today we will rally*
support for a Native American Vets Memorial.

We've been there, every conflict, but we have
no place of honor.

The discharge that disqualified him was not
dishonorable. Unique, certainly, but not a stain.

No matter. It was his story. He told no one.

Within and atop the Gridiron Church

> *--Old Crow meets football's Chief Osceola and his horse*
> *Renegade, and we later stumble upon a Hall of Legends.*

We strolled onto campus, past the stream
of youthful warriors and young empresses
treading to morning classes, speed-
walking. They were stoked on
boiled coffee and
apple muffins.

No one gave
us a second glance
as we meandered to our
destination, a place I couldn't help
but think of as the Gridiron Church
on the hill, a place of stained glass

logos and brick walls taller than Trojans

had stacked at the Dardanelles
channel to keep out the Greeks.

Greeks circled the church,
a stadium of course, the bowl
that hid the field that had its own tall posts.

We found a wall of glass double doors
and stopped our meanderings. We entered.

Crow pointed at the Seminole paraphernalia
and almost smiled. *Who should bet
on this? A gift shop!* He kept walking,
and we followed until we reached a wall
of locked glass doors with grass beyond.
Crow gently shook each handle until
he found one loose and then nudged it
open onto the grassy bottom of the bowl.
A pale horse and rider pranced within
the nearby endzone. He dressed
in native gear; it was clear
he was an Indian Chief.

The horse wore a banner across
the flank that read *Renegade!*
and high-stepped as if a
Lipizzan stallion having strode in
from Austria. The chief pulled

on Renegade's reins. *Who are
you-all?* he asked. He stared.
This is a private rehearsal.

Crow nodded. *I am John Jumper, Cowkeeper,*
Billy-Panther, but named at birth
Ochafanwaw, the blackbird king,
the ancient Crow. And so, who

are you? The freckled kid on horseback
now seemed puzzled, unsure, even
a little nervous. Was he Greek?
Was he Seminole? Was he Poli-sci?

I'm Chief Osceola, he said. The horse
cried, a high-pitched call. Crow
nodded. He glided to Renegade
and stroked his neck; the beast
calmed. He looked Osceola
in the eyes and squinted.

Osceola, chief of the Seminoles,
said Crow. *You ride a horse well.*
He whistled and Renegade turned
statue-still. *I am chief of the Calusa,*

and you look nothing like Osceola.

The kid fell stiff in the saddle.
His face grew sullen. He frowned.

Antonia and I wavered at the back
of the endzone while the two Chiefs
stood first and ten at the ten.
For these moments, it was as if
we'd never existed. We were unknown.
Unknowable.

Slide off your horse's back. I will ride him,
said Crow. And the kid obeyed. Sat Indian-
style at the nine. We knelt. Old Crow

and Renegade sprinted to the far end's
goal post, circled it, then galloped
to the fifty. He and the horse waited

at the midpoint. And then they slowly
trotted back to us. He jumped off
and handed the reins to the kid.

Thank you, said Crow. Next, the old guy
shuffled up to the boy and pulled
feathers from the turban, the two long
black ones. He left the white. He jammed

them into a pocket. The kid said nothing.
As we made our way back inside
the church, Antonia whispered to me,

*Osceola could be his son. They looked
so much alike.* I shrugged, gently rapped
the hickory stick against my ear. I stretched.

Maybe I was waiting to become a panther.

Crow boarded an elevator, waved to us,
and we followed. We rose to the top.
We found a long, empty hallway—all students

now in their rooms—with plaques
and display boxes full of photographs
and bio notes and quotes.

We'd found the Seminole Hall
of Legends. Did it celebrate a single

one? I scanned the wall for natives.

We walked slowly, as if tourists
in an ancient cathedral or a narrow
museum. Antonia studied the display

of Norman Thagard, the first astronaut
to ride a Russian rocket to space. I glanced
at the tribute to Faye Dunaway and a write-up

of *Chinatown.* Crow paused a moment
at the Jim Morrison box and his story
of meeting a Muscogee ghost

after witnessing a car crash as a child.
But then Old Crow parked himself
beside the large and bright display

of gridiron and acting god Burt Reynolds.

Crow absorbed the posts, scanned
each photo as if reviewing a holy text.
At this point, Antonia and I stood

just behind him. I read the bio note.
It says here he was only ¼ native,
not one-half like you said.

Crow said nothing. He was too busy
feeling the heat of the star, I supposed.
The hallway was getting cold.

Antonia said the air was musty.
The cabinets needed dusting.
It reminded her too much of tombs.

My Johari Window

*   --More reflections on my inscrutable classroom lectures
at Seminole Tech while we ride the inscrutable elevators of the
Gridiron Church.*

Down in the elevator we tumbled
within a narrow, vertical tunnel
inside the gridiron church.
Just before we entered, a professor-type

with an almost-garnet tie and jacket
whisked past, and Antonia said
*Look, there's your double. He looks
a lot like you, especially the nose.*

I disagreed. Mine was somewhat crooked;
his was straighter. We maybe had similar
hair. The doors slid closed. We tunneled
downward, one of four elevators headed in

the direction of the slightly west,
Soul's Town, as Crow had mumbled
that night beside the fire. Two boxes
stayed up, two slid down. I could

now see them as the four panes
of a window, my Johari Window,
something I'd once and always explained
to the kids of Seminole Tech, as a tool

for communicating with those not
like you. *Intercultural interaction,* I'd said,
*is very difficult, full of shocks, but if we
think in terms of frameworks, we can*

see the different styles and learn the roads
to compromises. The kids looked blank,
but curious. I'd draw a window on the chalkboard.
Four panes, four boxes. Half the class,

Black and Hispanic kids, leaned forward
in their desks and focused. Others were glassy-
eyed. In each square I scrawled a word
Arena, Blind Spot, Hidden, Unknown.

These four exist between me and you. But how
much that's hidden of my inner self depends
upon the way that self's been cooked
within the stew of country, heart, and home.

Thus, is our private self more public or private,
depending on where and how we're bred? I said.
They shrugged and wondered who fought
within the Arena. *No fight. That's what's known*

between you and others. They asked, How blind
was the blind spot? Would it see a sucker
punch? *No, that's what others know*
about you that you don't.

They shouted, "But *that's* the **unknown!**"
Perhaps, but it's also what neither you
nor the others know. They cried, What's
the hidden? *What you keep close.*

Keep close to the heart, the guts, the jaw. I
pointed to each to make my point
perhaps too forcefully. One student
stood, still stuck on *unknown,* and said

If it's unknown to both, why pretend
to know it; that's the window corner
with a crack in it, *idn't?* A hole.
Class dismissed. A Haitian woman

stopped to query about homework; her
t-shirt read: *The Only Potatoes We Eat
in Apopka Are Fries.* The elevator
was slow in the gridiron church.

Perhaps it took us into a hole that led
to a basement or Soul's Town or Hades,
the truly mysterious. And perhaps the man
in the almost-garnet jacket and tie was my

almost-unknowable self. I suspected
Antonia owned my blind spot. I couldn't
figure my own math that made me *me.*
I might write an equation on the board:

Filter = Message + (2 x Noise) + (Meaning/2).
I was a cipher to myself. I would never
find my place if I never found
myself. But it wasn't that simple. I needed

my own private formula. *I = Noise
without Meaning divided by soullessness.*
In this moment, I so wanted to be
the panther. A big cat could care less

about the unknowables. So true of a child too.
Sometimes I'd wished my freshmen were younger.

The elevator's doors opened.

Crow led us to sunshine.

Mission (Part 1)

> *--How Old Crow, Antonia, and I trekked to San Luis
> Mission, toured the gallery and grounds, and found Chief
> Buffalo ready to continue the furious stickball game.*

Old Crow hypothesized that an old goalpost
might await us and Buffalo at the Mission.
Or at least the well-hoofed ballfield might
have been cleared since the last bad cyclone.

He considered it as good a destination as any.
I'm not sure why, perhaps because he seemed
so confident, but neither Antonia nor I argued.
We left church and headed to the Mission.

We abandoned the gridiron ballfield for another,
a field more pure meadow than grass measured
by hashmarks and logos. We abandoned one hill
and climbed another. We must have seemed

a strange trio trudging along the roads, roads Native-
named, Pensacola, Ocala, Tennessee, until we scaled
the parking lot that dead-ended only yards
from the Council House. Crow was home.

Antonia studied the palm-thatched roof
of the Mission San Luis de Talimali. And the fort
that housed the soldiers of Madrid and Toledo.
I was disappointed to see no goalposts

because I longed to hand the hickory stick
back to Crow—I'd tired of holding it.
But stickball seemed unlikely. A bald eagle
swooped down to eye us but then disappeared

into nearby woods. The sun crept higher.
Inside the Welcome Center I found a painting
of Apalachee playing the game; they were painted
in white lime chalk or black stripes. I showed

Crow how they batted the deerskin
with their hands. They used no sticks.
He nodded. *They kicked, swatted, butted,*
he said. *But their aim was the same. The game*

changed when the Muskogee-Creek arrived.
The older tribes' ways morphed into blends
of rituals, blendings of peoples, a broad mix
of voices and songs and ways to mark moonrise.

An afternoon full moon edged the treetops
outside a window. Antonia slid past a giant
photo of an eclipse and paused at a painting
of Calusa men spearing seatrout at the water's

edge. She studied the placards full of text,
the history of this southwest Everglades
tribe. *Crow?* she said, *don't you have*
a name in your Native-tongue?

Didn't you say it was Ochafanwaw?
And Crow answered, *Oh yes, and John*
Jumper or Cowkeeper or Billy-
Panther, depending on weather.

But yes, I am the blackbird king,
Ochafanwaw. Antonia nodded. She
pointed at one beige placard with black
letters, then knocked a knuckle against

the hard surface. She puffed her lips.
In 1568—which is, I believe, well before
the blend with the Seminoles—it says here
a missionary kept close to a King Carlos

in Escampaha, the heart of the Calusa
empire. How did a Calusa king get
a Castilian name? Ochafanwaw strolled
to her side and stood stone still.

No, he began, *this is chief Caalus. The Jesuit*
Rogel, who lived among us, called Caalus
a cacique, a prince of his people; other Spanish
must have confused his name or the tribe's

name, and decided the "Carlos"
sounded close enough. I slid behind them
and spoke like a clan-man from the academic tribe,
Classic case of cross-cultural misappropriation.

They both ignored me. *In Cuba,* she began,
cacique is the word for a hotshot politico.
This plaque makes it sound like your Caalus
accepted the name King Carlos. Held it close.

Crow said nothing. He stared at the painting
and smiled and inched closer to the frame. He
pointed. He glanced back at Antonia. *Do you see*
this woman here, just a few feet behind the chief?

That's his beloved sister. His closest confidante.
Do you see her? Look closely, lean forward.
Antonia seemed annoyed, but studied the figure
standing behind the Everglades King.

And you truly see, don't you? asked Crow. He
gestured with his palm. *What?* she replied.
He laughed. *Why she looks exactly like you;*
so much so, she could be your sister.

Crow turned to me and glanced and nodded,
as if we'd given her a good dose of her own
version of *misappropriation*, her game back at
campus of mis-identifying doppelgängers who

roamed the school. Antonia grumbled, then walked away.
Old Crow spread his arms to either side, as if stretching
before a game to play. I still had his hickory stick,
but he'd not shown interest, seemed happy to roam.

At this moment, all other Mission-goers remained
within the Welcome Center's walls. We three had
rambled outside to a strange stillness, the atmosphere
thick with more than hillside humidity.

Was it raining? But the drops did not make us
wet. The air wavered, but it was not midsummer
sun-fire heat. The wind no longer held traces
of petrol; instead, every smell was full green.

The sky was loud with birds, so loud it felt
as if a megaphone had been planted inside my head.
Did the ground tremble? No fault lines hid
beneath these hills. My brain simply spilled.

From a break between two mighty oaks
a howling stretched the limbs and then
a rumbling grew. It was Chief Buffalo.
He knew what to do.

Crow snatched the stick from my pocket
and dashed to the meadow between the palm-
thatched house of God and the Council House.
Buffalo charged, the deerskin ball balanced

securely on his stick as if glued. Old Crow
wished he still chewed it, but he'd coughed it
clean into his rival's clutches. And Buffalo
charged to a faintly visible pole that appeared

near where I now stood, the pole clearly a ghost.

The War of the Ghosts

> *--A story I told at Seminole Tech to explain how Bartlett's
> Schemata theory developed from English people's recalling
> of an old Native American folktale.*

One night two young men of Apalachee
went down to the Wakulla to hunt sea cows,
and while they were there it became foggy
and calm at the springhead. Then they heard
war-cries from underwater. They feared
enemies! The pair escaped to shore, hid
behind a cypress log. Canoes came up
from the springhead's cave, and the two
heard the noise of paddles. One canoe
glided up to them. There were five men

inside, they said: "What do you think?
We wish to take you along. We are going
up the river to make war on the Spanish
people." The tallest young man said,
"I have no arrows." They said, "Arrows
are in the canoe." The tall boy said,
"I will not go. I might be killed. My relatives
do not know where I have gone. But you,"
he said, turning to the other, "may go with them."

I'd pause here to tell my class how Bartlett
had deliberately picked this tale from a culture
much different than the English. He wanted
to know what subjects might recall at term's end.

So one young man went, but the other
crept home. And the warriors followed
rivers downstream to the Fort San Marcos
de Apalache. The soldiers charged
to the Confluence of Rivers and began
to fight, and many were killed, though
they too were ghosts. In the midst
of battle, one warrior spoke: "Quick,
*let us go home: **that Indian** has been struck."*
The young man thought: "Oh, they are ghosts.
Their arrows are not real." He did not feel sick,
but they said he had been hit. The canoes
slipped back to the Wakulla, and the boy
went ashore to his house and made a fire.
He told everybody and said, "Behold I
accompanied the ghosts, and we went to fight
Spanish people. Many of our fellows died,
and we killed many defenders. The ghosts
said I was hit, but I did not feel sick."

And then a red stew and a black cloud
spilled from his mouth. The red seeped
out for hours and hours, then vanished.
At dawn he was still. His people buried him.

Mission (Part 2)

--Then a vast ballgame of ghosts of the Apalachee ensues
with Crow and Chief Buffalo at center; elaborate tales of
ancient Apalachee gods, chiefs, and warriors—Nicotailjulo,
Nicoguadca, Ytonanslac—reveal the game's origins.

Ghosts seeped up from the ground.
Dozens and dozens and dozens,
as if a blooming burst of common
chickweed, white flower after white
flower, some black striped, others
wound with red and yellow cloth.
They were Apalachee, returned to
play after 400 years delay.
They seemed prepared for war.
Their skin was translucent, but
they stood real and ready to strike
a buckskin ball. To even the score.

Of these ghosts, two teams appeared,
massive in number, at times fifty or
even one hundred or larger,
these men with painted skin running

shoulder to shoulder and wearing stray
feathers weaved into corded strands
upon their heads. Their weightless feet
pounded the grass into a dusty field.

Buffalo sprinted into the sea
of men, the deerskin balanced
on the end of the stick. He charged.

But the ghostly pole had faded into
moonlight, and Buffalo seemed
chagrined as the warriors danced

like wolves and howled like children
caught in voluminous storms. Crow,
too, slalomed through the maelstrom
of Apalachee people. Clouds gathered.

Within this Day of Ghosts, the hours
slipped backwards to before the game
had begun. The pole now hammered
together, sassafras pegs pounded into

the triangle at the top. The crowning
eagle's nest was like the barrel of
the crow's nest, like Old Crow's nest
speared by the foremast of the Santa Maria.

The men and women used grapevines to raise
the ball pole to stand as tall as a Calvary cross.
One young woman dragged a ball stick
through the grass to spin and begin

a ceremony to celebrate Nicotailjulo, mother of
Nicoguadca, the patron god of thunder, rain,
and the game. Old Crow and Buffalo danced
to and fro, one wanting a goal and the other

desiring denial. They fought over the ball
and then a scalp replaced the buckskin. So
they fought over that. The skin stretched
as they both tugged and pulled, the hair

becoming wiry. The ancient ghost of Ytonanslac,
the game's founder, shrilled with honor as the pole
settled into its hole. And then someone tossed
the deerskin fifty feet skyward. Buffalo sprinted,

his stick chopping air; Crow chomped
at his rival's heels; the hickory whirred. More clouds
gathered. The thunder boomed as one big drum.
The deluge would soon unfold. The Apalachee

performed their final rites of love and blood
and broken bone. The music droned to a hum.
Soon the clay field bled the color rhône.

Antonia and I knelt beside the Council House
and fell speechless; the Ghost Day's cold winds
sliced our minds and bodies like a steady knife.

I was unsure if we were in this new world
or outside of it. The Apalachee did not see us
but saw Crow. Or maybe they wished to not
disturb us or guessed that we had nothing
to offer in a wager on the outcome of the game.

Some stars of the ball begged women for love
because of all they'd sacrificed to train and gamble
on the game they couldn't lose. *Yes, they'd bet it all.*
(Old Crow's claim too. Was this his guide
for the game?) Thunder now rattled trees. If one
held up his palm would one woman's small-boned,
calloused but delicate hand accept it? Rain came.

Antonia reached over and touched my hair.
You're wet, she said. *You too.* I nodded.
Her dark eyes blinked. *This dream
is real.* I cleared my throat. *Or we're
ghosts too.* The rain was steady but not
hard. Lightning lit the distance.

Mission (Part 3)

> *--A continuation of the vast ballgame of ghosts with
> more stories of Apalachee gods, chiefs, and villages—
> Eslafiayupi-Nicoguadca, Ochuna, Ivitachuco—divulging
> the game's roots. Subsequently, the gridiron Chief
> Osceola and the professor-in-garnet revisit Old Crow and
> me.*

The hot light lit past stories, the tale
of a grandfather keeping his grandson
safe from Chief Ochuna who feared
this boy would kill him, this boy
born from a mother impregnated in
some extraordinary way and lost
and found by a panther, bear, and blue
jay. Ochuna told the boy to search

for flint in a deadly spring. The child's
grandfather knew the danger so gave him
shell beads the boy could hand a diving
little bird to safely find the flint.
When the boy survived the dive,
the Chief declared *the first* ball game
—a game designed for dying!

On the field Ochuna tossed the buckskin
towards the sky midst a pile of players
bunched together like spikes on a pine cone,
and, as violent as any gridiron kickoff, they
stomped across each other to be the first
to reach the plug. A dozen, later stretched
out like tuna across the clay, baking
in the cruel sun, breathing heavily,
marked the first injured of the day.
But the boy prevailed, and on the winning
score his throat cracked thunder, and then
all knew he was lightning-flash Eslafiayupi-
Nicoguadca, born of the sun.

Another flashing bolt stopped time
to reveal the era of 1662, when the War Chief
at the Mission challenged the Peace Chief
of Ivitachuco for a game,
the message brought by a man
wearing raccoon tail, red face,
and ray-like stripes as black as night,
as, to any friar, a look as deadly as
the devil's. And when the War Chief
won, it was as if god had struck a bell,
because soon the Spanish were undone.

But only to return again
as did the plagues they
brought, fevers more fierce
than lightning, lungs aflame.

The Mission ghosts, young
though dead, sprang to chase
the deerskin, and outpaced
older Buffalo and Crow, who
gasped and stood with hands
on knees. Their sticks sat
near their toes. The ball
screamed across the sky,
a comet racing time to
win the game of universal
endings, never-ending stopgaps
in this continuum unweaving.

Crow stood near us
and shook his head;
he couldn't catch
his ball or breath.
*When these ghosts
tire, then the game
is ours,* he said. But
he seemed doubtful.

The rain grew harder.
Lightning knocked
the sky but oddly
the thunder lessened.
At the end of the glade
a man on horseback
now appeared, as if

a warrior in a movie
scene. The ghosts
ignored him. He at
first seemed brave
but then full lost.
The water bounced
from his new feathers
as fast as flintstone sparks.

The gridiron Chief
of Seminoles strode
upon the scene, young
Osceola, his war paint
melting, his face obscene.
He could not fathom
this field of ghosts
not dreams. Renegade
neighed and shivered
in the rain. Crow
approached, and the boy
now looked relieved.
The Calusa man held
the horse's reins but
stared at the boy and
blinked. *You are me,*
said Crow, *a possible
impossibility. But you
have my nose, my jaw,
my eyes.* The boy
said nothing. The old
man lifted Osceola
off the saddle and
dropped him gently
to the ground. *I will*

*give you back to your-
self,* said Crow. He
removed the chief's
hat and garnet robe.
You now are no longer

me.

    The boy was wide-
eyed in the rain. The
game continued as
ghosts savaged ghosts
in beautiful chase and
translucent blood. We
watched the two, we
spectators to matches
we did not understand.
The boy took the horse
by the reins and wandered
southeast in the direction
of the football church.
Crow picked up his stick.

The kid passed by
another coming from
the coast or campus
or parts unknown,
but neither nodded
to the other. *It's **you**,*
Antonia said, *your
double from the college,
your reflection in
a mirror darkly.*
Yes, a professor-type

looks less regal in the rain,
if he ever did. Soaked through,
his almost-garnet jacket stuck
to skin like glue. His nose
was perfect, mine askew, but
his mouth, hair, and rounded face
made a perfect match for mine.

At this moment, the ball near-
scraped a corner of the triangle
that signified the pole's near-
top. The Apalachee howls
now only grew. The game
would never stop.

Buffalo sat beneath the post
and watched and waited.
Crow stood by us and tapped
his hickory upon the ground.

The professor approached
and with great formality
shook my hand. *I understand*
you are the man who knows
"culture" like the back
of his hand, he said. *I taught*
it once, I replied. *Good to know;*
I do as well, downtown at
Enormous State. I had no
reply. No one had ever heard
of Seminole Tech, so why
even try. *And I'm always keen*
to learn others' methods
for cross cultural communication

within multinational business
operations. I nodded, said, My kids
came from all over. Guatemala,
Mexico, etc. My double pointed
his finger to the sky.

The ball flew high, but he aimed
to make a point and saw not
the ball but only his own words.

Let's say we meet a Mayan
in Cancún, Mexico, and we
know something of Mexico
but nothing of Mayans,
so we use our schema
based on appreciation
of Hispanic norms to create
a first version of this culture.
So our culture, Culture A,
knows not truly Culture B,
our Mayan friend, but only
B1, a version as incomplete
as a pie plate with only
one slice. But A may not
realize this and assumes B1
is B, a pie fresh baked
and whole. But the crust's
not crisp and berries are
hard, so we must realize
we must build B1 upon B2
upon B3 until we can make
our way to the schema full-B.
Thus, you see the matter,
with building vital schemata.

I'm unsure of your mixed
metaphors, I said. *The pies*
and all. But I'm thinking
Mayan is not Mexican
so not necessarily Hispanic.
And you're example worries
me too. My kids got
the schemata matter
best, when I simply
told them the story
"The War of the Ghosts."

What's that? the professor
asked, a worried but challenging
look that was his mask
upon his face.

I explained, but as I did,
the man slowly backed
away, and checked his
watch at every pause
until he faded into rain.
I stopped.

He had no time, said Crow.
Or too much of it, said Antonia.
Both, I said. *And maybe that's*
why I had to leave the college.
The moon grew rounder. The ball
streaked past us. The ghosts
of Apalachee dug toes
into clay as they sprinted
toward the pole.

Mission (Part 4)

*--How Chief Buffalo creates a chance to score, but Burt
Reynolds (Bandit) steals the show to prevent a second
shot. And Buffalo scolds Crow on his military discharge
which may be more shameful than Crow is admitting.*

Both Buffalo and Crow stood
and jogged toward a pile
of players crushed upon the ball.

The warriors tired, and perhaps
these chiefs saw their chance.
Some players came to the side-
lines to eat the ghosts of foods
past and present, maypop, palm
berry, cabbage palm, knotweed,
and cherry plum. Some plants
looked delicious to me and
Antonia. We were less sure
of what they'd done with corn,
the lye-hominy porridge made
with ashes, the thin gruel they
called *onsla*. But the ghosts
gobbled the transparent meals
and returned to the game ready
to smack the ball
to the top of the pole.

Ghost posts began to waver
into being along the edges
of the circular ballfield. I
stuck my hand through one,
puzzled to see thirteen poles,
short in stature compared

54

to the center-of-circle
tall goal standing
fifty feet or more. Antonia
stood beside me now and
whispered, *Crosses.* Her
Spanish relatives had tried
to tame these people with
their Mission, and because
the Apalachee died of plagues
of Old World origin
and the Spanish didn't, the
natives, not knowing better,
believed the Hispanics had
better magic than their own
Chiefs. The Chiefs saw this
handwriting on the ochre wall
and acquiesced to Catholic
rites and Jesus-owned beliefs
that this one good god gave relief.
The crosses glowed softly
white along the infinite
horizon of the ballfield
lit by springtime light.

And then a horse cried
in a roar, a noise from
an equine throat that
sounded more like
a rumble. Boy Chief
Osceola's beast had not
returned, that was clear,
and, I realized, did horses
rumble? An angry look
scraped across Antonia's

face, as she pointed to the
east. The ghosts' jaws
dropped to the ground
without a sound; they
froze in terror. Chief Buffalo,
seeing his chance, followed
the now bouncing ball and
took a mighty swing. Crow
raced from the right but
could not stop the stick
from popping the buckskin
sphere so very high.

The triangle awaited him,
hanging solemn like a mask
a Calusa might have made.
The air whistled.
We paused and stared.

He missed! Buffalo's face
fell from glee to pissed!

And then the horse revealed
itself, appeared from mounds
of dust, sped onto the field,
spun donuts in the clay,
its rider laughing loud above
the horsepower bray.

The beast was Antonia's Mustang
we'd abandoned yesterday
in Miccosukee, stolen by a madman
in a hat. *It's
Bandit!* screamed Old Crow

with a bellow, then a laugh.
Impossible, but yes, the phantom
of Burt Reynolds snagged
the ball as it plunged downward
on its arc, and made one more circle
around the pole, left Buffalo crying
in the clay, and then the Bandit
made us eat his dust and zoomed
away.

Crow turned to me. *You see,*
he's on our side. He has
the power to take us
to the top to honor
and restore
what all's
been
lost.

I did not understand.

You see, said Crow, *only he*
can make the chiefs of
Washington rebuild

The
Council House
and reraise the stone,
the circle that recalls our dead
in spirits flying overhead the D.C.
mall that makes all our peoples raise
their chins to celebrate as we once did with
mounds of shells and clay and bones and stones.

He has the voice they'll
take to heart ... and believe!

But Chief Buffalo stomped
in front of us three
and pointed his mouth
not at me or Antonia
but Crow, and he yelled

You with your dishonorable discharge
will burn in hell. No natives can now
achieve the rebuilding that we'd hoped
because too many like you, especially
you, have made us foolish in their eyes.

Buffalo ran in the direction that Bandit
took, and Old Crow stood and stared
at the clouds of clay still drifting
in the air. The ghosts, the post, and
crosses had vanished into ground.

Do not worry, said Old Crow. *Buffalo*
doesn't understand or care.

Attan and the Green Corn Dance

      --Of the circumstances of Crow's discharge in Afghanistan.

In the arid country of Afghans
Crow found himself missing
the Everglades. There were
hours of peaceful boredom,
days even, but then moments

of sheer violence that shook
him worse than the bark
of any alligator—that was
the story of Afghanistan
in his year of duty. No water.

No M-16 on his shoulder
this evening. He and two
Anglo G.I.s walk a street
and see dancers in a circle,
and hear music, mostly drums.

Near the Everglades, that's
where he learned the Green
Corn Dance with his Seminole
and Miccosukee people, his
one uncle, tall as a tree, always

whispering to him that he and
Crow had to have Calusa blood
because *No Indians get this tall.*
Only Calusa. Even the Spanish
said so. Crow takes it firmly

into his heart, and this Pashtun
dance on a dusty street in dry
Afghanistan strikes his blood
with fever. The drums, so like
a Corn Dance beat. The women's

dresses, unlike yet like Seminole
patterns, colors. Like his dance
the Attan is all about circles,
and when two men in black
whip pirouette after pirouette

he can't help himself. He dances
too. His comrades try to stop him,
but he makes tight circles around
the spinning pair and they
keep turning and the crowd

expands like a balloon, until
it's bulging in all directions.
Things seem un-right to two
G.I.s, one who runs to track
down a commanding officer.

But Crow is deep in it now
and can't be stopped. His
Sergeant and then Lieutenant
shout at him to desist, but he
ignores them, and the crowd

grows louder and pushes the
officers to the perimeter. It takes
M.P.s to finally crack the spell,
to take the Green Corn Dance
out of the Attan and make him

sit in the brig until he can
Start speaking some
English! Start
making some
sense!

National Native Memorial for Veterans

--A description of what rests within the D.C. National Mall.

A giant stone circle, a section
of a pipe made of granite, a ring
for a giant's hand, the opening
of a tunnel to hell, he thought,
when he saw the flames stretch
from the bottom to top, and since
war is hell and the memorial
is mostly remembered for Veterans
who died in it, maybe the tunnel
is the best metaphor since it marks
a passage underground. One circle,
a ring, balanced on its edge within
one after another partially enclosed
circle. A standing ring atop rings
within rings of granite then boulders
then stones. This home for memories
welcomed the world to 2020, a year
with two auspicious ovals. Crow
was there, searching through lists
of tribes, some chiseled into rock
and others soon to make their mark.
He closed his eyes and dreamed
of Afghans, Pashtuns, Attans.

Tribes

*--Of the tribes listed on the National Native
Memorial for Veterans.*

Crow searched and dreamed.

Augustine Band of Cahuilla Indians, Rosebud Sioux Tribe, Apache
Tribe of Oklahoma, Bad River Band of the Lake Superior Tribe of
Chippewa Indians of the Bad River Reservation, Quinault Indian
Nation, Big Pine Paiute Tribe of the Owens Valley, Passamaquoddy
Tribe, the Ak-Chin people, Pit River Tribe, Burns Paiute Tribe,
Seminole Tribe of Florida, Sac & Fox Tribe of the Mississippi in Iowa,
Quapaw Nation, Prairie Band Potawatomi Nation, The Muscogee
(Creek) Nation, Houlton Band of Maliseet Indians, Pascua Yaqui Tribe
of Arizona, Ione Band of Miwok Indians of California, Miccosukee
Tribe of Indians, Kickapoo Traditional Tribe of Texas, Ho-Chunk
Nation of Wisconsin, Eastern Shoshone Tribe of the Wind River
Reservation, Navajo Nation, the Haudenosaunee people, Hoopa
Valley Tribe, The Osage Nation, Eastern Band of Cherokee Indians,
Fort Mojave Indian Tribe, Inaja Band of Diegueno Mission Indians
of the Inaja and Cosmit Reservation, Elem Indian Colony of Pomo
Indians of the Sulphur Bank Rancheria, Federated Indians of Graton
Rancheria, Crow Tribe of Montana, Los Coyotes Band of Cahuilla
and Cupeno Indians, Comanche Nation, Cold Springs Rancheria
of Mono Indians of California, Zuni Tribe, Citizen Potawatomi
Nation, Winnebago Tribe of Nebraska, Twenty-Nine Palms Band
of Mission Indians, Wampanoag Tribe of Gay Head, Tonto Apache
Tribe of Arizona, Santo Domingo Pueblo, Thlopthlocco Tribal
Town, Rappahannock Tribe, Inc., Three Affiliated Tribes of the
Fort Berthold Reservation, The Seminole Nation of Oklahoma,
Pueblo of Santa Clara, Nez Perce Tribe, Match-e-be-nash-she-wish
Band of Pottawatomi Indians of Michigan, Little River Band of
Ottawa Indians, Jamestown S'Klallam Tribe, Iowa Tribe of Kansas
and Nebraska, Delaware Tribe of Indians, Chickahominy Indian
Tribe, Absentee-Shawnee Tribe of Indians of Oklahoma, Chicken
Ranch Rancheria of Me-Wuk Indians, Alabama-Coushatta Tribe
of Texas, Fort Independence Indian Community of Paiute Indians,
Hopi Tribe, Klamath Tribes, Mashantucket Pequot Indian Tribe,
Lovelock Paiute Tribe of the Lovelock Indian Colony, Omaha Tribe
of Nebraska, Samish Indian Nation, Oneida Nation, Penobscot
Nation, Tuscarora Nation

On the granite,

no Calusa.

Commander in Chief

*--Of the vandalizing of National
Native Memorial for Veterans and the news
report that referred to Natives as "Something
Else."*

Late 2022 the National Native
American Veterans Memorial
was defaced, devastated, toppled,
scalped by bats, hammers, crow-
bars, paint, and every square meter
received a mark of hate. What was
the who and why? A low on the dial
radio show had noted how in Wisconsin,
a state the current President won by 20,000,
82 percent of Menominee County,
home of the Menominee Nation,
voted for him. Bayfield County
home to the Red Cliff Ojibwe
gave him a win too. Navajos
in Arizona, where he won by
just 10,500 votes, voted 84
percent for him, the 67,000 people
of Coconino, Navajo, and Apache
Counties. The man on the broadcast
ranted how the people had lost
their old Commander in Chief because
of these Indians. The people'd pounced
on D.C. once and lost, but on
December 29th, the anniversary of
the Massacre at Wounded Knee of
1890, the end of Indian resistance

to U.S. military might, the
insurrectionists, inspired by voices,
guided by radio, raged, raided,
and ransacked, leaving the memorial
a wreck of steel and granite and stone.

And so, a new Commander in Chief
rode out from the wastelands. Did
he note how the news revealed
on CNN that 6 percent of the nation is
Something Else? No, not the White,
Latino, Black, or Asian, but the slim
2.8 million who went to bed Indigenous
on a Tuesday in early November
and awoke the next morning
as *something else*, something
like a Nation, but more, though
still struggling, still restless,
still waiting.

Return to St. Marks (Part I)

> *--How Antonia and I debated the virtues and
> shortcomings of Smokey and the Bandit II, and how we
> three came upon the Big Dismal sinkhole and faced the
> Long-Ears-of-the-Sea.*

That pendejo! shouted Antonia.
That motherfucker stole
my Mustang!

Crow briefly raised a palm.
He'll return it. He's native,
and he's come to help.

He's dead, I said,
again. Crow shook his head.
He is our Indian Bandit,

growled Crow and laughed.
He handed me his hickory stick,
and I wrapped both hands

around it. Antonia had calmed.
She looked thoughtful. *He was*
wearing that same hat in some

posters for Smokey and the Bandit
II, the one with the white-feathered
emblem on the band, a snake-skin Florida

in the center, a tiny silver star on the east
coast. I sighed, ready to roll my eyes.
You're back on your anti-consumerism

rant? Your unfinished dissertation
you left behind in Cuba? But Crow
was rapt, so she continued. *The film*

is all about greed, a $400,000 **bet**
(Crow's eyes grew wide with
the word) *for Bandit to get an*

elephant to a convention in Dallas
in three days' time. They could care
less about the ruin in their wake

because it is all in the name
of the money they'll make. Crow
whispered, *What did they bust?*

She said, *A gigantic roller coaster.*
Fifty cop cars, fifty tractor-trailers
too. A million rules as they sped

from Miami to Texas in their
brand new 1980 Pontiac
Trans Am, the "Son

of Trigger," as they call it. (*No, no,*
Old Crow whispered, *"the Son of*
Golden Cloud," the sprinting palomino.).

Well, I quipped, *you might have a point,*
but I doubt anyone intended that
interpretation to fly. She pointed her

finger at me and said, *And the Anglo writer*
Patrick Wensink also writes
a similar thesis, you'll want to know.

I sifted the name through my mind
and frowned. *Wait a sec, Wensink*
is on an anti-capitalist bender?

Isn't he the guy who wrote the book
with a quasi-Jack Daniel's label
plastered on the cover? The one

who got a cease-and-desist from
the bigshot subsidiary? And then
watched his book hit #1 and bragged

his path was the best new model
for big-time publicity and fame?
Antonia shook a finger at me.

He never bragged, she said. *In four days*
his book fell from #1 to one oh
two. His tiny publisher,

Lazy Fascist Press, closed shop
five years later, never to print
another word. I shrugged.

That's a lousy name for a book-
maker. Crow pointed south and said,
No matter, we must return to St. Marks.

We have no Mustang or Palomino,
so we must walk and find a spot
to spend the night again.

Why did we head south?
Crow insisted on finding
the Spanish ships that docked

at St. Marks. From there, riding
winds toward the Keys would
be faster than chasing a Mustang

on foot. Who knows where Bandit
might ride, but Crow suspected
that Big Cypress might draw him

down the State, especially since
his early-career guest roles
back in '61 included a jaunt

on *The Everglades* where all
the extras were played
by Seminoles instead of red-

faced white men. Buffalo,
stuck on foot, would take days
to scour the state.

We'd started late afternoon,
so by the time it was nearly dark
we found ourselves at the edge

of Big Dismal, the largest sinkhole
in this county named after Ponce
de León. Crow led us down

a narrow path that slowly wound
its way to the water one hundred
feet below surface where we drank

huge mouthfuls of coldness
from the aquifer that tunneled
even deeper into ground.

As we crouched at water's edge
a strange smell leaked
from the surface, a stench

like stagnant and muddy seawater
left in a fetid bucket, as if the foulest
mildew crept past

the metal rim. Old Crow slowly
raised himself to standing. Antonia
and I turned our heads askance.

He watched a bubbling at the center.
In the gloaming, the dim light shone
enough to make shapes clear

just beneath. A giant thing with black
triangular pectoral wings methodically
flapped a lazy path to the sinkhole's

whirling transparent middle.
It stretched thirty feet from tip
to tip and had a horse's long and stringy

tail. Upfront, its eyes were hidden
by horn-shaped cephalic fins that
pointed forward like insect antennae.

Just behind the horns trailed long
mule-like ears. It had skin like
bear fur and a row of wolf-sharp

teeth. The creature most closely
resembled a manta ray, and Crow
seemed truly spooked.

We-waw Hycko Capko! he said.
He started up a different path
and waved to us in panic.

The beast had sunk, no longer
visible at the surface. *I know
a place where we can hide,*

*but we must hurry before it
gathers up its venom
and whips us with its tail.*

He stopped at a crack to a cave
in the rock about forty feet above
the water and squeezed through.

Antonia and I hesitated, but then
Crow stretched his hand
and pulled us in, as if returning

us to womb. We stooped within
and waited. *It's the Sea-Wolf,
the Long-Ears-of-the-Sea,*

he whispered. *We can't have it
bite us or lash us with its fringe.
It carries deadly plague. One*

wound could spell the end.
He glared out the fracture
and darted his eyes to find

gift-light within the rising full moon.
My one uncle, tall as a tree, told me
Seminole have tales of Long Ears,

the Hycko Capko, the dire wolf
with the deer-like legs, but we
Calusa have the devil-ray,

the water-born Long Ears,
the Sea-Wolf that preys along
the dune-line as we might gather

coontie roots for flour. I peaked
through the crack too, trying
to catch a glimpse of dark wings.

But mantas live in the sea, I said.
Crow frowned. "*Yes, true. This one*
is born of bad magic and bares

the mark of Chief Buffalo. Did you see
the curled ivory that defined
its horns, like bison of the Paynes

Prairie of Ocala? I pondered
this legend, this creature of fable.
But I wondered why we hid in a cave

from a creature that lived in the water.
You will soon see, said Crow with awe
and pain in his voice. Then,

like gentle rain, a dripping, dripping,
dripping. The light fell darker,
and I peaked at the Sea-Wolf

lifting itself above the water,
flapping its wings in gentle gusts,
somehow hovering above the pool

as if it was normal within the laws
of nature for so little movement
to keep such bulk aloft.

Its long ears behind its horns
gushed water as if spigots,
as if its hungry thoughts leaked

out as soon as they were dreamed.
The huge manta floated just
outside our cave, its hairy

tail partway in the water. Its curled
buffalo horns glowed in the moonlight,
and seemed as dangerous as a boar's

infected pair. We were trapped
in the tiny crevice. We barely had
space to stand. The wings eclipsed

the crack. All was dark.

Talking in the Shadow of Wings

Crow seemed unsure
if the Sea-Wolf would
eventually tire and drift

off or sink. We sat in a circle
and said little. The air
stank more of a fetid sea.

It hovered like a gigantic
hummingbird with slow-beating
feathers, as if waiting to dip a long

beak into a feeder. But all that came
from its toothsome mouth were growls.
The drips continued as it gently

flapped its wings of furlike skin.
Crow wondered if it might fall
asleep while floating, the soft

wingbeats rocking itself to slumber,
like frigatebirds he'd seen
in dreams. I peered at the beast

and said, *You're dreaming.* Antonia
sighed. *He could be right,* she said.
Let him dream. I could hear its breath

shudder through its grill-like gills.
We wait, said Crow, so we did. We
talked story. He told us of shells

piled high to the sky and a woman
he helped care for after her leg
had been snared by a shark.

He'd waited on her as her calf
slowly healed, brought her fresh
water and oysters and clams.

He held her when she had night-
mares of teeth breaking skin
and muscle. She shook

as with fever. After two
months, she was healthy. They
stayed together for two months

more, but then he had his tour
of duty and never saw her again.
Antonia spoke of her abuela,

how she liked to sit on the screened
porch on the hottest days. The grand-
daughter would bring Cachito over ice,

the Sprite of Cuba someone had
smuggled through mysterious ways.
She'd wipe her abeula's chin again

and again with a soft handkerchief
made of silk and cotton and embroidered
with a capital A. The humidity beaded

along the jaw, and Antonia worked
to keep her comfortable as she
rocked on the creaking boards of the house.

I had Seminole Tech in mind again. Those
students haunted me like the ghosts
of ballplayers who circled Crow's thoughts.

The War of His Ghost

*--A retelling of the Native American folktale by one
Englishman in 1915, months later in the experiment, which
helped exemplify Bartlett's Schemata theory.*

*Two Indians were out fishing
for seals in a bay, when along
came five other Indians in a war-
canoe. They were going fighting.
"Come with us," said the five
to the two, "and fight."
"I cannot come," was the answer
of the one, "for I have an old mother
at home who depends on me."
The other also said he could not come,
because he had no arms. "That is
no difficulty," the others replied, "for
we have plenty in the canoe with us."
So he got into the boat and went
with them. In a fight soon afterwards*

this Indian received a mortal wound.
Finding that his hour was come, he cried
that he was about to die. "Nonsense,"
said one of the others, "you will not die."
But he did, and his tongue fell out,
and as he opened his mouth
a black thing rushed from it.

Bartlett's Schemata

> *--From a memory of one of my impenetrable classroom
> discussions at Seminole Tech.*

Of course it's gonna change,
she said. *Who can remember*
all those weird details? And
the story's too long anyway.

I was trying to explain Bartlett's
study, hoping to get them to
get the *why and what* of schemata.
From the back row came soft chatter.

But how has it changed? I asked.
They looked at me glumly, said nothing
for a minute. Then: *Ghosts dipped. They*
left the story. No ghosts. The boy,

who'd told me during office hours
he worried he might be
gay, looked pleased with himself.
Confident. All seemed well. He was

onto it. A dressing mirror leaned
against the back wall, perhaps left
by the previous professor's class.
Near the mirror a black woman

raised her hand. *The guy's
got a sick mother. I don't think
he had an excuse before to miss
the war.* A tall Apopka dude coughed

then said *He's not killed by a ghost
arrow. It's real. And it seems to kill
him faster. There's no campfire either.*
I smiled. *So what's the **why**?*

The first speaker replied, *It's like
I told you, too many weird details.
Who's gonna remember all that?* She
sounded annoyed; I was wasting her time.

*No one has a perfect memory,
one month later after reading
it twice.* I nodded and said, *But how
has memory changed the memory?*

She pursed her lips, puzzled and
puzzled. *Did the Indian have a memory?*
she asked. I wanted to sigh. Another
day of teaching the pitfalls of Culture A

hoping to communicate with Culture B.
Intercultural business communication, I'd
called it. How one from one world speaks
to another from another. They were

interested but stumped. Or anxious.
*So how did one culture, the English of Bartlett's
study, interpret and retell the tale of the Indians?
The English folks wanted logic to guide the story,*

*people to have clear reasons for decisions,
the narrative to have no magic. They recalled
what the words had captured within the context
of their own culture. It's hard for people to remove*

those built in . . . glasses. The backwall's mirror
showed the classroom's clock above
and behind me. It was time to go. The boy
from office hours waited for the room

to clear. He didn't stand. *I'm thinking,*
he said, *they'll never see the truth of me,
as if that me is a left-out ghost.* He blinked.
For a brief moment, I swore

I'd disappeared from the mirror beside him.

Stickball against the Long-Ears-of-the-Sea

> *--Of how Old Crow, Antonia, and I battled the giant Sea-
> Wolf manta ray.*

Crow was right, the Sea-Wolf
now floated in suspended
animation, asleep at the wheel

of time. Crow squeezed from our hole
in the throat of the sink and gathered
sticks. He noted a hole above us

like a chimney, smiled, and lit
a fire. The air was now chilly
so we were glad for the heat.

He left again, scaling
the rocky wall like a Billy goat.
He returned with stones, a bit

smaller than the size of my palm.
He dropped the rocks
in the flames. They grew hot.

Doña Antonia? Crow asked. He
handed her a large, flat stone the shape
of a long face, gave her a damp branch

to hold. *Can you please push these
rocks onto this stone plate and then
bring them out to where we'll now wait?*

She complied without question. Crow
and I crouched on the ledge by the crack
and waited for her to bring the plate

of hot rocks. We faced the wall
that was the Long-Ears-of-the-Sea
as it slept on the job and snored

like a baby. From a deep pocket
he pulled two thick gloves and dropped
them beside me. *Use these,*

he said. *And give me my
stick.* I was glad to be rid of it
because it'd scraped my spine

as we sat in the cave.
Antonia appeared with the rock plate
in her hands. The half dozen stones

glowed like the eyes of a scallop.
*Pick one up, toss it up in the air,
a little to my right and not out in front*

and then stand away. The tight gloves
could feel the heat of the stone I pulled
from the plate, but I could handle them

without pain. I made a gentle throw,
and Crow swung with the force
of a gale, and the rock cracked

off the stick and arced to the Sea-
Wolf who now raised an eyelid
that drooped. A fire sparked above

a gill slit and left a red mark, and the
long ears of the beast started to spring
straight to the night sky and waver

with obvious shock. *Another,* said Crow.
We gave it a second go, and the stone
popped beside a buffalo horn

and made the manta grunt and moan.
Three more times Crow smacked a rock,
and each time he started a fire

on the skin of this monster. The thing started
to rise, as if lifted by steam the stones
made below as they hit the water

and sank. *Now you,* Crow said. Off-guard
but obliged, I let him wear the gloves
while I held the stick. He tossed it, and I brought

the hickory back past my ear, my triceps tightening
to ready the blow, the rock drifting down
to the ground, and then whipped my hips

and my arms in a spin and pummeled the sphere
near sun-hot and now turning. It stuck
against the Wolf's skin, then peeled off. Long Ears

gave a shout! All the air whistled out
in the blink of a red-embered eye, as
a balloon speared by an arrow.

The monstrous manta collapsed and plunged
to the sink and crashed to the water and soaked
us with spray. It fell into darkness, the dark

of the aquifer, and now we three were free
to climb from the throat of Big Dismal
and make a safe camp for the night.

Return to St. Marks (Part II)

> *--Old Crow finds us work on a new replica ship for
> passage south, the Santa María de la Consolación of
> Ponce de León, and Antonia and I question why we
> follow Crow.*

First things first, Crow made sure
I'd hold the stick for the long walk
to St. Marks. We ate persimmons

and made good time as we neared
the confluence of the two rivers
just after noon. I held the hickory

as if it were a staff, imagining myself
a cowkeeper keeping cattle corralled.
At times I swung it with both hands

gripping tight as a two-handed
sword. *Crow, I said, we've been swinging
this stick like a bat, like baseball bat.*

*Shouldn't the ball get launched from the
tip, more like a King David sling?*
Crow pursed his lips.

*The best magic can make the difference
when dealing with ghosts
or beasts. And with driving off Long Ears,*

*I didn't want the firestones to burn a hole
through the handle or the cup's leather web.*
I held it lightly now and asked,

*And don't southern tribes play with two sticks
not one?* Crow glanced skyward. *Buffalo
and I play a private* game, *a ceremonial ritual.*

Our rules bend the rites and make them too.
I shrugged, shook my head, and Antonia
patted my shoulder. *We're in a New*

World. Don't try to explain it, she
sighed. We looked up and saw
the docks

of St. Marks. The *Niña,* the *Pinta,*
and the *Santa María* had sailed
but now tied up at the port

sat the *Santa María de la Consolación,*
the proud ship of Ponce de León.
A carrack by type, it could carry

enough to feed a small village
or two. Crow said he'd worked
it before, and we'd do so again;

he only needed to talk with *el capitán.*
Crow went on his search, and Antonia
and I sat in the shade by a porch.

What irony, she noted staring
at the forty-five meters of wood.
Our Mother Mary of the Afflicted

brought Ponce de León's crew
to afflict the natives with their
cruelty and war and disease. I tossed

a shell that bounced off its
forecastle, and the bow seemed
to groan like a half-hungry bear.

Only a moment, then the noise
of lapping returned. *What makes*
us stick with him? she suddenly

asked. *I was looking for something*
to do, I suppose. Professoring had left
me feeling exposed. But I've not yet

found direction as the Crow flies,
but something tells me he has
an answer to give so I follow

and hope he can show me a way.
Antonia stared at a mullet below
as it swam to and fro

and kicked the water with
her un-shoed feet. *What about*
the Professor-in-garnet? Did he

give a clue? she asked. *Certainly,*
I said. *I know a place at Enormous State*
would only make me feel smaller

than small. She launched her own
shell at the ship of León and struck
a grey rope and left a white mark.

I'm searching for family, my heritage,
as I've said, and I too think Crow
has something to do with what

I shall find. That painting at the Mission
haunts me still, and makes me half-
dread how sailing on this Santa María

might leave me afflicted. Five gulls
appeared above us and screeched
their hungry songs. A manatee breeched

and snorted a call and sank into sea.
Crow reappeared with a smile. *Let's go
win!* he said. *Our work papers are set*

and soon we will sail. He gently
removed the stick from my back
pocket to press a thumbnail

against the handle where a burn-
spot now lingered. Satisfied, he handed
it back, and we boarded.

Stick

          --A meditation on the stickball stick.

almost 2 to 2 ½ to 3 feet long
hickory or pecan
bent in a loop at one end
—in some games, the loop is laced
       with deerskin or squirrel skin—
sometimes adorned with purple martins' plumage,
       crested flycatchers' feathers
handle wrapped in blackened cowskin
       or maybe 3 bands of black ribbon tape
       and a thin rope band or sometimes
       in a pinch
       black duct tape
       for quick repair
ball-cup is 5 to 6-inches long, 2 to 3-inches wide,
       1-inch deep
to find a stick look for hickories

on hillsides that don't get
        a whole lotta water
        and the grains are tight,
        the wood is strong
cut it on the new moon; and fast after that
        you can just bend them
        and won't have to boil them
        and bend them
some games played with two sticks, some with one
from a twelve inch thick trunk,
        a log three feet long, you will waste
        nothing, you will make thirty-two sticks
when you cut that trunk, you will bring it down
        slowly into nets, and until that wood is
put into play, it will never touch ground

To Calusa Country

      --In which a mirror image of our Santa María de la Consolación appears, and we three witness Ponce de León's final skirmish with the Calusa.

We floated to the gulf and south
on the *Santa María de la Consolación,*
listened to Crow tell a tourist, onboard

for the trek, the struggles
and successes of Ponce de León,
the explorer extraordinaire always

looking so wan. Did he thirst much
for youth? *No, mostly treasure*
Crow said to the man from up north.

In 1513 Juan Ponce de León was first
to make contact with the Calusa.
He found them

unfriendly. In 1521 he tried again
to plant a colony in southwest Florida,
but the Calusa

were caustic. We traveled on his ship
that had failed to succeed
in satisfying his greed,

a gold-lust spurred on by his
conquering of San Juan and
the Tainos he'd forced to farm

and mine by way of pike, sword,
and matchlock rifle. We sailed toward
Key West, charting a way to Fort Myers.

The sky clouded, pushed down with dark
upon the masts of this Santa Maria. All fog.
The tourists slipped below deck.

Crow, back atop the mast in the nest,
scanned the churning horizon until
it released from the fog

a double, *Santa María's* doppelgänger.

The fog released it, and the
horizon churned with one
mast and atop, a crow.

A second *Santa María de la Consolación*
drifted toward us, as transparent
as glass. The blackbird, *ochafanwaw*,

gave a slight caw, and this soft song
brought upon that deck a crew
as translucent as spring water.

And there stood Juan Ponce
at the forecastle looking proud
and determined and ready to

trounce. But from the east
came canoes and canoes
and canoes. Warriors

and holy men, some in wooden
masks of south-slash-pine, skimmed
across the sea faster than

flying fish. Their forms were as faint
as those fin-like wings. The carrack's
soldiers watched and waited and loaded

their rifles. *Oh my God*, I whispered,
This is truly it, Bartlett's story
of natives. This is

The War of the Ghosts. Guns exploded.
Arrows flew. The Calusa chanted
and hooted as if owls fiercer

than stikini, the deadly owl-witch
of the woods, and the Spanish lit
their small cannons scattered

across the deck. Could ghost-explosions
kill specters? Could spectral-explosions
kill us? At this point, our *Santa María*

was ignored. Perhaps we were more trans-
parent to them than they were to us. Everything
stank of gunpowder. We somehow could smell

their sea-cold blood. Arrows lodged in Conquistadorian
necks. Shafts struck water, a rain
of sticks. Blasted Calusa legs sank to the bottom

strafed by clouds of hammerhead sharks.
Were the fish ghosts too? And what lessons of
schemata could we learn from this mess?

Did the Spanish revise their Schema A
notions of Calusa to Schema Z
where their minds preferred to see all

Calusa as dead? Did Calusa see not schema
but schemes that drove Spanish to plunge
in over their heads? And what of

the culture of spirits? By what rules did
the after-living have to make values?
Crow had climbed down from the mast

and stood beside us on the aftercastle,
the stern of the ship seeming safer
than the pellets and arrows that streaked

past the bow. The Spanish were dropping,
became ghosts of the ghosts
of the dead. The spectral *Santa María*

started to turn to the gulf. From the largest
canoe, wearing the largest mask made of cypress,
a shaman now stood, his face distorted by black

stripes and off-kilter eyes; he bellowed,
then sat, and a Calusa archer rose, his bow
as big as the most giant rod that could grow

on the shell mounds that stood
tall as hills. The shaft launched, screamed, shook,
then bent downward;

the arrowhead was
a black eye's much blacker pupil. It came down
like a curse and struck Juan

Ponce de León in the thigh. The point
was a tongue full of white sap.
Ponce would soon die.

Manchineel tree juice had lodged
tight in his blood; even with the arrow
removed, the blistering dug through his bone.

The man and his ship flew back to the fog.
The Calusa cheered then fell silent.
They'd spotted our ship.

Crow dashed to the bow
and started to yell. But Seminole
didn't sound like Calusa.

The canoes streaked forward
as if shot out of hell. I didn't think this
would end very well.

Mounds

> --*A description of the Calusa's manmade island
> and capital, Stababa.*

A good-sized pile of dirt beside
a hole dug by several tall men.
Or piled earth atop a grave.

Or clay and debris stacked high
near a village, some built as small hills
in flat landscapes for ceremonies

and eagle-eying. For the Calusa, they made
an island with their colossal mounds of shell
and bone and the broken shards of life.

Call it Mound Key, but for them it was Stababa,
the capital of Escampaba, the kingdom of
the Caalus. The Calusa.

For the Spanish, they called it maybe Caalus
or Calos, then temporarily, it became
Mission San Antón de Carlos, but

later simply Estero, or no. That was
the town on the estuary near the isle,
the key mostly forgotten to the shadow of time.

They lived sunsets in the shadow
of these mounds, this island,
this way of living, this universe.

Stababa Chronicles

*--How Old Crow, Antonia, and I avoided battle
with Calusa ghosts, jumped through a time-space portal
that resembled a manta, and stumbled upon a meeting of
Calusa and St. Augustine's Spanish settlers at the Native's
capital, Stababa, leading all to wonder at these expanding
Impossibilities and Immensities that may cause this entire
Adventure to be considered Apocryphal.*

Crow demanded his stick
from me. He climbed a mast
and drummed the hickory

against the Old World pine in a rhythmic
roll. Long needles flew from the canoes
that approached, but Crow kept trunk

between himself and the arrows. Had he
lost his mind, caught between cultures—
ghost, Calusa, Spanish, Anglo—was he

surrendering amidst *The War of the Ghosts*?
I scaled the post to shake him awake
or discover the purpose behind

his fast pounding. *What are you doing?*
I yelled. *We should go below deck!*
He wrinkled his brow. *No, we made*

good magic back at Big Dismal, so now
we will call the Long Ears of the Sea.
I now knew he was mad. We were lost.

Take this, he said, and gave me the stick
and showed me the pattern to pat
on the pine. I gave him a look, but then

did what he'd showed me. *Louder!* he said.
Thunderstorms of arrows crashed through
the air. We kept our heads close to the pole.

Just below on the deck, Antonia crouched
at the foot of the mast and shot me
a questioning look. Crow spread his arms

open, gripped the post with his knees and sang
to the sea. Ghost-weapons scraped his skin
as he chanted, not hitting but making him

wince. I drummed harder. In the gulf, a good
fifty yards from our ship, the sea crackled
as if the water were earth and a split

had divided one blue cresting crust from another.
A crack formed on the surface, and Calusa
stopped moving, their eyes filled with dread.

Harder! Crow said. So I hammered the stick
as loud as I could, the noise like a woodpecker
army assaulting a hollow tree in the forest.

The harder I hit, the wider the break in the ocean
became, until it burst like a wound full of blood
and dead skin.

The horns of a manta the size of a live oak
rose through the tumult until the beast lifted
high, became a giant black diamond hovering

beside us, shading the ship as if a sail from the mast
of a great pirating vessel washed up from hell.
Crow waved his fist, glanced at each of us,

and cried *Jump!* And we did.

Into the black void, into the Sea-Wolf,
the dire manta dog of the gulf, the Long Ears
Crow had tamed, the *We-waw Hycko Capko,*
this leap became
the latest thing hard to explain
on this journey of our
confused and unhappy trio looking for
exit from *The War of the Ghosts.* We
did not desire a *black thing* that might

crawl from our mouths in the dawn, so
we felt glad to be long gone, but
where did we go?

To jump into a huge, black-furred manta
must seem quite insane, and Long Ears
it *was* as it had been at Big Dismal
floating above the surface like a T-Day
Gotham Parade balloon ready to drift with
the wind. But as we each crouched to spring
concurrently from the *Santa María*
of Ponce de León, the colossal black diamond
transmogrified into a corner of space
filled thick with red stars and planets of gold.
It was a doorway between times and places,

zones and inner-worlds trapped within
outer spaces, and it swept us full backwards
onto what seemed towers of star-white shells,

Stababa of Escampaba, the kingdom of
Chief Caalus, the self-made island of
Calusa, the peninsula's *fierce people*.

We three stood on the edge of the tallest
ziggurat, flat-topped pyramid, bright white
plateau, a shell-strong mound forty feet

high, forty yards long, and forty feet wide.
These structures defined the seascape,
these juts of land made by hand

by a determined people, this island
of middens. We saw *where* we were,
invisible to two thousand Calusa

and a few hundred Spanish, but *when*
were we? Crow whispered to us as he
pointed at the tall, black Calusa chief,

his skin dark with tar-paint. There stood
Caalus (*Chief Calos, Carlos, King Carlos*)
welcoming the short Spaniard from

Saint Augustine named Menéndez
de Avilés, the main man of north
Florida. Near 1566 polite Avilés

made a deal with Chief Caalus
to marry the sister who always
stood by his side, who the Spanish,

mistakenly, thought was one
of his wives, and this pact
would keep the two sides

from warring like Ponce de León
had once tried with these
non-Catholic people.

And we three ghosts of the future
stood amongst these ghosts of the past
and watched the masses grow upon

the enormous bone-bright midden.
Menéndez and his men marched, 200
soldiers with their ready *arquebuses,* rifles

packed to shoot natives and perhaps us
if we became ghosts these ghosts
could finally see. We stood as quiet

as the waters that lapped the island
and watched five fifers, ten trumpeters,
a dozen drummers, and one man

strumming a psaltery. A loud
dwarf danced and sang; flag bearers
flapped their fabric bearing

the Cross of Burgundy. The Spanish troops
trod the ramp that led to the mound's top,
to the chief's house roofed with cabbage

palm fronds. The house stood 30 feet high
and fifty yards long. Some soldiers gripped
their guns tightly in both hands. Would they

fire if the Calusa became bellicose? Or if we
three became visible? I stood tensely, even when
a chorus of Calusa teens sang,

tall women of a height just
shorter than Caalus's sister
who, though not her brother's queen,

stood beside him as an unspoken
next-in-command. His wife sat
nearby on a throne of bone

and yellow pine. Inside the great
house, the singing continued, the dancing
began, and the dwarf joined in

and banged on a can he'd kept
in a pocket. From my own pocket
I pulled the stick to return

to Old Crow, and he took it and became
corporal in this unfamiliar past; a Calusa
handed him a welk-shell cup full

of yaupon tea, and he drank it. Feathered head
-ornaments and body paints
and shoulder-straps of cowrie coils

made the dancers seem angels of the earth
fresh from sand and sky. The Spanish
didn't notice Crow, instead eyed helpings

of fish, roasted and boiled, oysters and clams
and sea grape jams. And fell entranced by
the dancers. To my surprise, as if flashed

to life from a strobe appeared Chief
Osceola and the Professor-in-Garnet. They seemed
ghosts too, or maybe a bit corporal with a hint

of spit and hair. Osceola, though junior,
looked younger than young, and my professor
appeared at first deaf and then dumb. They twirled

and the boy bounced to Old Crow, but my friend
pushed him back into the crowd with a sigh. He
kept gliding and vanished beside throngs

of Calusa who cawed. My man in sharp garnet
stopped beside me and whispered, *But who
will you teach? Only you can get through*

*to those kids. I myself would still argue
your voice needs to be heard.* He clasped
the hand of the dwarf who mumbled

a song, and together they danced, not doubles
but close, as he looked more
or less like me depending on lighting,

and Osceola and Crow seemed more shadows
than mirrors. But where did Antonia go?
She stood next to the sister, Caalus's true

Queen, the woman whose life would control
the rest of this dream. And if not for the feathers
atop her long head, I would not know

who was who, who was live and who dead.

1. Twins A1.

*--A Seminole folktale concerning twins and thunder
and lightning.*

*A baby boy was born and somebody killed
the mother,* said Josie Billie, son of Ko-nip-ha-tco,

one day at Big Cypress at the dusk before
D-Day. *The afterbirth was tossed aside,*

*but it came to life. It was wild and lived
in the woods. The father knew nothing*

*about the wild boy. His little boy, though,
ran and ran and talked to the wild one.*

*One day the two boys got on the backs
of white horses and just kept on going.*

*They soon were bored, so they shot
an arrow into the sky and it stuck fast.*

*So they shot themselves up as well.
A cloud god came over to find what made*

*the noise. He let them stay as long as they
married his sisters. They had lots of kids,*

*and all were bad kids. That's why our
children are frightened of the boys Thunder*

*and Lightning, because of the terror
they flash and crack from the sky.*

2. Twins B1.

Within the Johari Window live
the Blindspot and the Unknown.

Two of three of one Calusa's
souls are Shadow and Reflection.

Is a double what's always been there
in your Blindspot? Or is your double

what's always been there
but completely Unknown

to you? The Calusa must embrace
the Shadow and Reflection

of one body inhabited by souls, including
twin spirits, the same shape, but one

dark and the other light. Is the Shadow
then the Blindspot, the dark place in

the peripheral vision? And the Unknown
the exact Reflection that was so much

like you . . . you never noticed it? We are
blind when we live in shadows.

When we reflect, we see how much
we do not know, and that's the unknown.

If your Reflection runs through water
with your Unknown, how wet will each

twin become? If your Shadow hides your
Blindspot, who will seek out and note

your true twin? But when the Johari-believers
meet the Calusa people, the children

all look alike. They play hide-and-seek
in the thunderheads and stay out of sight

in the shadows. When it rains, they spot
their reflections in the puddles. The twins

are all but unknown to themselves
and each other; since the images

are all alike, they do not know who
is who. When you meet both

your souls, one Shadow and one
Unknown, you will hear their

voices through fractured glass
and finally know your own.

Stababa Chronicles Continued

*--In which we three witness Chief Caalus' sister Doña
Antonia, wife of St. Augustine's Governor Menéndez, set sail
for Cuba, and Antonia and I stumble upon another fizzure in
the time-space portal and are dragged onto a slave ship.*

Caalus's sister was christened, as requested
by Menéndez, and named Doña Antonia.
And now, finally, our Antonia stood beside

her doppelgänger, and saw through this window
the fate of her unknown family-past. Because
here on this wedding day her husband

had decided she'd sail to Cuba to a nunnery
to become a better Catholic wife, a way of life
she had no interest in. *See how the two women*

walk hand in hand but with frustration
that burns their faces, I thought out loud.
Crow seemed not to hear. When would

this ship appear? Our friend walked in shock,
not knowing where she tread as her slightly taller
half took them down the shell-walled

pyramid's ramp to the sea. All this doubling
and doubling echoed across the water, and I
could feel a trembling in the atmosphere

as if every molecule of time and space
were breaking because two versions
of the same universe scraped together,

the reason for endless twins. And here again
is where the gulf grew grim, a storm,
a fog, a downpour drenched the air.

Thus, another time, two ships appeared,
but neither was a *Santa Maria,* and each
was distinctly different, these imperfect

and ugly twins, each with a mission,
one bad, one worse. Each crew
with a dearth of moral code or decency.

One full of Spanish en route to Havana,
an embroidered cross on every breast-
bone, a bed prepared for a former

Indian Princess now a Governor's Wife.
The other ship came from a future,
one hundred years after this wedding,

and it filled with Creek and Yemassee
egged on by the England people
who favored a whip to the back

to make men work for free.
But where were we? Crow danced
with his Calusa, not noting the ships

now staining the horizon. I followed
the Antonias down to the water
and stood just behind my scholar

who now seemed more lost than grim.
These twins divided from each other as if
zygotes within a womb, so Doña Antonia

boarded the galleon, and my Antonia
was pulled across deck boards
of a British vessel that searched

for slaves. I grabbed her
hands and shoved aside ghost-men
more solid than wood. Their hands

were like sandpaper and now gripped
me tight and tossed me aboard
as day fell to night as Antonia

and I knelt in a cage and prayed. We
were good stock for slavers who'd
maybe sell us to Georgians or high

class Virginians or wherever our bodies
might fit. The ship sailed south. Neither
they nor we now seemed specters;

the blood on our arms was too real.
They swung arquebus-like, flint-
lock and Brown Bess muskets,

heavy guns on this 200-ton *Hesgeth*-like
ship. Stababa's shell-walls had faded
to background, then vanished.

We now knew we were
banished from our *own*
space and time

Bridges

       --Of my and Antonia's time upon the British slave ship.

Why had the Creek and Yemassee
moved us to the bridge of the ship?
They were kinder, at times, than the Brits
who maligned our existence,

but their kindness was thin, as in
a small sip of water or a fragment of
biscuit. I heard these men whisper
of *making for the islet* but first

they'd pass through the Keys.
And so, when the Natives
had left for the stern
the English stared at us, unsure

if we were Calusa or Spanish
or convicts. We had to be
one of those three to justify
our futures lives in slavery.

They kept noting the lightness
of our skin, and how this might
bring the best price in the end.
When we tried to speak, to argue

our case, all fell to the weird,
because our words made no
sense to them though our vowels
were the same. They laughed

at our gibberish, ignored our
pained faces. To the south
we sailed, the drizzle still
dropping, the fog still topping

the masts. We drifted between
the never-now and nothing,
or so it seemed. The sails
were full but we felt

stuck in ice. The crew didn't
notice, struck up old songs
and dirges, repeated the lyrical
bridges too often, too long. I tried

to complain—the tunes drove
Antonia insane—but all I got
for my efforts was an oar
to the nose that busted

the bridge and left me bloodied
and aching. My nostrils
poured red. My head was a halo
of pain. Antonia spat at the slavers

but they ignored her behavior
or laughed. They also discounted
the weather. The fog became black,
as if exhaust from a tailpipe

of a more modern machine.
Did an engine's rumble
wrack the air? Did these men
not hear nor care? Were we,

Antonia and I, a *nothing* paired?

1. Twins A2.

--One of my shorter—Thank God!—meditations.

Noble natives nab natives
to be sold into slavery.

How does this give us a new point
of view, to move us from A1 to A2?

This hands us something to not
exactly appreciate but perhaps

points to new paths to communicate?
All learning leads us to ameliorate,

it's said, mostly by those
gone or now dead.

2. Twins B2.

--A history of how the Spanish saved the last of the Calusa.

Ignoble Spanish rescue Calusa
at the tip of the peninsula

from Brits and their native slavers,
the Creeks driven south

from the wars between England
and Spain, endless raids on the sites

of their middens. The Spanish,
in 1704, open a door to the sea,

to take the last of Calusa to Havana,
not heaven, but not slavery. Two hundred

died from disease. Did the last dozens
re-see these Iberians as friends, who

seemed less like B1 and more like B2?
The final Calusa fought fading. We did too.

New Bridge

> *--How Antonia's Mustang reappeared, and how she and I
> escaped the slave ship.*

Brit jaws dropped. Creek and Yemassee
crowded the stern, thinking to jump
before the bad magic hit the ship
with a *clunk!* Between two keys

a bridge had appeared, clear now
despite the fog, made of cement
and bright steel. If the ship did not
turn, all three masts would be clipped

and become broken sticks. All halved
and sails torn and askew. *Where in God's
name?* one fat Anglo had murmured,
And by who? A tall first mate replied,

*Don't know. But that bridge's all armor
and stone. Its makers, unknown.* Natives,
though ghosts, assumed ghosts were
the builders. They yelled for the Brits

to reroute the ship. Instead, a roar
like one thousand panthers echoed
from the crossing, and there then appeared
a white Mustang from hell or just maybe

heaven, for Antonia and I recognized the guy
at the reins. It was Burt Reynolds. A smile
on his lips, his white hat set straight,
he screeched at the midpoint and made

to reroute our fate. He seemed at his Bandit
best, and only needed horsepower to then
do the rest (just like the old Sequel). He'd not
be like Smokey, get caught between spans

of a drawbridge. No, he'd perform tiptop,
like riding that elephant in downtown Miami
or driving past struts of a rollercoaster's frame,
leaving it unscathed, while his rivals found

rough going as the structure caved,
then toppled and collapsed as if Troy.
Bandit's clearly the hero, and he guns it,
and the Mustang leaps from the road

to the deck of the ship and lands
near the bridge and screeches then
stops beside the main mast. All sailors
fly to water; tailpipe smoke circles.

I tumbled into the backseat, but Antonia
stood by the driver's door to browbeat
Bandit to give up the wheel; after all,

it's her car; and she assures him, she's

the much better driver. He resists for a beat,
but then shrugs and slides over, and soon
Antonia is racing across the planks as
two ship masts strike the bridge and topple

to the aftercastle, supplying her tracks
for the Mustang's tires to follow. She steers
for this exit ramp, screeches up like a train car;
Bandit grabs his hat before it blows off; and I

clench my teeth and pray to the cross, though
I'm barely Catholic. The Mustang rockets up
with Antonia flooring the pedal to send us all
soaring onto the bridge of the Keys, old U.S. 1,

the Florida Keys Overseas Highway. We
head north to Miami, racing out of the fog,
the drizzle, the never-now of the ghosts;
however, Burt Reynolds, who's most

surely dead, seems more alive than he did
in the Sequel, now wearing his Bandit smile
like a badge. And where has Old Crow

landed? We paused in Islamorada, so I

could buy ice to numb my bent bridge.
My nose was so sore, I had trouble
smelling the salt air. The sun was
bright and made us all squint.

I kept thinking about the slavers, and how
we seemed the only vassals aboard,
but in a War of the Ghosts nothing's
for sure. And again, how was Reynolds

more real than real as we streaked
towards the Everglades, the south-
east of Tequesta, the tribe the Calusa
had mostly befriended with a pact

that'd brought shellfish for all who
were hungry. North, we rolled, our
journey still turning. Bandit now
napping and Antonia speeding.

Pretendians

>   *--Reflections on those who pretend to be Natives.*

Antonia pointed out how the slavers
thought we were Natives. *But you
are,* I corrected. *You're clearly Calusa.*

*You looked just like Doña Antonia, as if you'd
caught her reflection and melded it to you.* She
passed a Jeep Cherokee, ignored double lines. *It doesn't

feel right,* she replied. *I'm Cuban, and to pretend
otherwise is a lie.* I sighed. If anyone had been faking
it'd been me. Never claiming, but maybe not

insisting hard enough that I was neither Native nor
Pretend Indian living a fantasy of others' rituals. *I'm
the guilty one,* I admitted. She said nothing; I said

I think I've always wanted my own Pretendian tribe.
Antonia sighed. *One thing I noted in my dissertation*
was that Burt Reynolds did not have one drop

of indigenous blood. I'd wondered that, but played
Devil's Advocate: *But it says he's Cherokee*
on his Wikipedia page! She glanced at him, then gave

me a look. I smirked. *But are all Pretendians*
bad? I countered. She said, *It depends*
what becomes of their game of pretend.

Little Havana

> *--Where we visit the Miami barrio, and I join a children's*
> *ballgame, and Old Crow returns to the story.*

Antonia veered her Mustang off
Federal Highway, past Calle Ocho,
and around to a side street.

She pulled into what she told me
was her favorite gas station
bodega. *I will grab us a six pack*

of ice cold Inca Cola and a big box
of torticas de morón. She blinked. *More ice?*
She climbed from the car and gestured at Bandit,

How can a man sleep for so long
on the road? She ran her hands
through her hair. *I may see*

someone I know in there; so I might
be awhile. I shrugged, not very interested
in a stomachache from cookies and soda.

I stepped from the backseat to stretch out
my legs. I figured she must have needed
escape after our own narrow escape; she

desired distraction a bodega might offer.
We actually had no destination, since
we'd lost track of Old Crow. We simply

didn't know where to go. Hispanic families
marched past us on the hot sidewalk, all with
glowing blue balloons and gifts for *un cumpleaños.*

I, suddenly curious, decided to follow; I
needed escape of my own. Cars' exhaust was thick
at times. Heavy. Unlike the bright red hibiscus

blooms lifting my spirit. Fast-spoken Spanish
showered the street, but I tried not to fear it.
I wandered past old houses, both tall and

small. Small porches full-stocked
with cerveza and glee, Cuban jazz
brass rocking the steps on CD.

I was glad to have my mind
free of Calusa, of Crow, of ball games,
and ghostships, of slavers and Seminoles.

I could now briefly be in the moment
and absorb old Miami and everything
that made it open and warm.

A six-year-old raced by me and gave me
a curious look; I caught my reflection
in a car's tinted window, and saw

my nose was less swollen,
my eyes were less red. I hoped I didn't
seem more brute than man, a frightening

creature crawled up from the sand, a mishmash
of ghost and Long Ears, and I doubted my double,
the professor-in-garnet, would resemble me now.

I looked up and saw I'd reached the house
where a gaggle of kids crisscrossed
the front yard in a wild melee. A colossal

birthday party game had exploded, improvised
by using and abusing every paddle known on Earth.
Some had Stream Machine ItzaMashers,

others Play Day Boom racquets. One little
girl swung a PaddleZlam paddle. She jousted
with a boy holding a Bashminton racquet.

A trio bounced backwards with hands
full of FlagHouse Lollipop paddles,
and two in the back flipped WhackyBall

racquets. All colors flew past, embedded or painted
onto wood or light plastic. All these kids, ranging
in age from five to near nine had invented

a match that grabbed all their focus. The parents
must have sat in the back, glad for the break,
and waited for the squealing to end

and thus the wild fray too. But they played on,
bopping a skin-brown balloon, keeping it
off the green lawn and half-thoughtfully

directing it to a round laundry basket
atop a wooden birdbath. One loud kid
gave me a racquetball racquet

and gestured me forward with a hoot
and a holler. Soon I tapped in too
and sent the sphere flying

higher than rooftops, and thus it slowly
descended. They gathered around in
a bunch as the balloon floated back

downward, and after a tussle,
encouraged me again
to smack it skyward, *orta vez, orta vez.*

This went on for moments, then minutes,
and the time sang elastic, as I joyfully dashed
among the small darting faces.

Why was I so ecstatic? I passed it to smaller
ones to dunk in the basket, and challenged
the older ones to race hard and bash it

maybe higher than I could. My gut felt
so happy, my head lifted higher. Maybe
the kids I should spend time with

should be smaller not taller, not the youth
of Seminole Tech, but the children
of grade school who didn't care about cool.

There you are! a voice stretched
from the sidewalk; Antonia stood
with her hands at her hips.

She grabbed a loose elbow, and I
dropped the paddle, and the kids
re-immersed into their fun battle.

She and I walked a block and then stopped
so she could show me
Old Crow atop an Andalusian

with hooves actively stomping
the blades of St. Augustine grass
growing next to the street. Some

drivers stared at the pair, but horse and Crow
ignored them. He must have borrowed
this beast from Menéndez Avilés, and leapt

through a hole between that year
and ours. And there he now sat,
gave the black mane a pat. He brought

the horse close and said,
We still have work to do; the game
is not over. There's the worn buck-

skin ball that we must recover.
I glanced at Antonia. *But Bandit*
must have it. But Crow shook

his head. *He has it stashed up coast,*
just north of Jupiter. And there
we must bargain for our half of the game.

By strange good luck, two trainers
of Escudero Pasofino School for Riding
stopped and admired the tall Andalusian.

In minutes, Crow had offered them
the beast, and we returned to the Mustang
with Crow and me in the back and Bandit

riding shotgun. Antonia steered us
onto I-95, and soon we were flying
to north Palm Beach County.

Doña Antonia

    --A history and meditation on Doña Antonia.

Antonia was there-
not-there with Doña Antonia,

sailing to Cuba, more shadow
than soul. They reached the shore

of Havana and there met a ghost,
Fray Bartolomé de las Casas

known as "Protector of Indians"
who arrived in 1511.

He said he could offer no help,
because his cries for compassion

for Natives had been squashed
by the governing men of Madrid.

So things had changed for the worse
since Bartolomé's time (protection fell

scant), but the need for Natives
to become Catholic remained

stronger than strong. Contrarywise,
Doña Antonia was more worried

about offspring, so once in Cuba,
despite time with the Catholics,

she awaited her chances with Menéndez.
After one especially long expedition,

he slept in a nearby inn. He awoke after
midnight to find her, candle in hand,

searching the room, even under the bed,
to see who might be sleeping with her

new spouse. He awoke and fast-talked
a tale that Knights of the Order

of Santiago could not sleep with
their wives for eight days after return

from a voyage. She was skeptical and
counted on fingers that two days had

passed, so she'd be back in six more
for sex. She needed to cement

the pact between Caalus and Spain
as she'd promised her brother; she

needed a son. Instead, Menéndez brought
her back to King Carlos (*Caalus*)

on the island
of Calos (*Stababa*),

and hoped all would be copacetic
again. But it wasn't, because King Carlos

had been tricked by Menéndez
to make peace with the Tocobaga

of Tampa, and Doña Antonia
scolded her brother for making

a deal with the most hated
of rivals. She returned to Havana

and remained for two years and
learned her brother King Carlos had lost

his big head. She continued her
countenance that had made her so

famous in the eyes of the Spanish.
Her composure and dignity, answering

others' pleasantries so discreetly and
succinctly, made her a marvel to these

men. Menéndez saw her importance,
intelligence and knew her full

of good sense. Now our Antonia shadows
her double and admires her being,

but feels frustrated with all that op-
pressed her. Antonia feels gladder now

that she's left Cuba and the influence
of Spain. Maybe America's not much

better, but here she's free to start
a fight that can fall hard onto heads

that must roll. Her fierceness
will take its toll.

Burt Reynolds Dinner Theater

> *--Where we three and Burt Reynolds (Bandit) visit a dinner theater in Jupiter and examine the lobby's revealing museum; subsequently, my teaching of a children's acting class inspires Reynolds to help Crow in the cause to rebuild the National Native Memorial for Veterans; and beats of the Green Corn Dance grow louder.*

We four arrived in Jupiter, Bandit
asleep again, Antonia having raced
us up the Interstate, Crow and I caught

in our usual circles of mis-
communication. Antonia's smart
phone has dropped us at

the parking lot of the Maltz
Jupiter Theatre where the plays
are shmaltzy but fun, as in *A Meat*

Loaf Tribute or *The Wizard of Oz.*
Bandit finally arose and shouted
There she blows! That's the baby

where I sunk all my cash!
He reconfigured his hat and his boots
and sauntered across the asphalt

to bask in the bright, white edifice
shadowing old A1A. *Ain't she*
a beauty! I stared at its walls

of glass and frowned. *But I thought*
you said it was named after you?
Crow put his hand on my shoulder

and a finger to his lips. *Well, at one*
time. But look at the legacy I've left!
He grinned. He put his hat on his chest

as if saluting a flag. Crow handed me
back the stickball stick. I sighed
and stuck it back in a pocket.

Let's go inside, and so Bandit
led us straight to the lobby. We three
trailed just behind. The joint

was empty; perhaps folks had split
for lunch. We cut to the left through
an opening and entered a large space

much like a museum. In fact, it *was*
one. And here the pix and plaques
revealed the history of the theatre

and Mr. Reynolds. *Built by Burt Reynolds*
for a cool $2 million, the Burt Reynolds
Dinner Theatre broke ground in '78.

Such celebrities performed on its stage,
Martin Sheen, Julie Harris, Judd Nelson,
Sally Field, Farrah Fawcett, Eartha Kitt,

Ned Beatty, Vincent Gardenia, Kirstie Alley,
Robert Hays, Marilu Henner, Ossie Davis,
you name it. And three times Mr. Reynolds,

the U.S.A.'s top box-office draw for a five
year span, starred! He also founded his one
true love, the Burt Reynolds Institute

for Theatre Acting and Directing. The words
told more, about the eventual closing and
sale to developer Otto "Buzz" Divosta

then to media kingpin Lowell "Bud" Paxson,
who donated it to Christ Fellowship Church
at the turn of the century. In 2001, the Palm Beach

Playhouse was formed—and the rest is history.
The Maltz Jupiter Theatre kicked off in 2004,
and now it's so large it's hard to ignore.

We lost Crow but found him in the next
display room, a celebration of Reynolds
with a Trans Am on the floor and photos

and movie posters telling us more.
Crow grew excited as he pointed
to wall after wall of the early career

of this actor of fame, with showstopper
name. Antonia and I studied the space
and connected the dots. Bandit had vanished.

A guest role in two episodes in 1961-62
in TV's *The Everglades* with local Seminoles
as extras wearing their traditional dress and

driving airboats atop the river of grass. From
'62 to '65, he played blacksmith and deputy
Quint Asper on *Gunsmoke,* a half-Comanche-

half-Anglo who initially appeared as an avenger
since white men had killed his dad. In *Navajo Joe,*
a '66 spaghetti Western, he played Joe the Navajo

fighting bandits responsible for striking his tribe.
Next, on TV for 2 years, he was John Hawk in *Hawk,*
a full-blooded Iroquois policing the streets

of New York in late 60s gear. In 1969
he starred in *100 Rifles*
as Yaqui Joe, a half-Yaqui, half-white man.

The Man Who Loved Cat Dancing came out
in '73 with Reynolds playing Jay Grobart,
an outlaw married to a Shoshone named

Cat Dancing. Their children become
more Native than white and stay
in the village with Uncle Iron Knife.

I'd never seen Crow smile so big.
Maybe Reynolds *was* a strong-
blooded Cherokee or something

close to it. He'd been half-
Comanche, half-Yaqui, and raised
kids half-Shoshone on film, was he not

half-Cherokee too? And wouldn't
that make him a unique kind of twin?
For if you come from two different

peoples, aren't you your own twin?
One Cherokee, one white, a biracial
delight, a goodlooking blend of human.

Neither Johari nor Bartlett could solve
the misunderstandings between one
from himself or one from herself or

they from themselves. All these doubles
and twins all caught up in the possible
changeling-trope of kill and replace,

but what if having a twin means one
protects the other by taking its place
and saves its own savior by swapping

out atoms in both time and space.
And there caught in a photo
Chief Osceola in the Burt Reynolds

display of his gridiron days at the capital.
Did a garnet-clad teacher standout
in the bleachers next to the endzone

in the very same pic? A door now
opened and Bandit appeared
and waved us to enter his most

favorite room. We swept through
the door to the Institute. Class
was in session. A dozen pre-

teens (and younger) sat on the floor
of a stage and listened to a lecturer
trying to engage them with dialogue.

The kids piddled with their laces
and went through their paces
of repeating the chat-chat

back. Bandit did frown. I watched
the kids carefully and could see
in their faces a desire to break

from the drone. Their fingers
were antsy and their toes
were all dance-y and their eyes

thirsted for more. Antonia put
her hands on my back and gave
me a gentle push forward.

The speaker had paused to find
his place in a book he had dropped.
I slid in front of the kids and widened

my eyes and launched into a stickball
mime, a game of a type, where I swung
Crow's stick in slow-motion to act

out a most critical play. I handed
the hickory to a boy seated in front
and continued my mime without

prop. He paused at first, but then joined
the dance, and he handed the stick to another
and then several stood tall and swung

at a ball that was not there but existed
for all. Twelve kids did rise and bulged
out their eyes as they swung at the ball

that was more shadow than pupil (the third
soul of Calusa) and twirled on the stage
and acted enraged because my role

had become protecting the pole
where scoring was not possible,
and I was the storm and the gale

with the mouth of a whale ready to
gulp every shot. The actors in groove
let faces grow hot, the slow-motion sprang

to fast and then faster, and finally we spun
at warp speed, and I wound up
with the stick. We hopped in rhythm,

and one six-year-old girl let out a yell
they made the un-hearable music shake
the floor more. When a small boy

scored, we all rolled on the wood,
and enjoyed the victory like we should.
That was great! said ol' Bandit; he seemed

more pleased than usual. *You're a natural*
with these little ones; we've got to get you
involved. The lecturer stood in a corner

and moved his head glumly. Bandit grinned.
I guess if you can soon make it back or maybe
sign a contract, I'd be willing to do whatever

*helps next. And by the way, what **was** that?*
Hey, don't count your bets! I can't remember
shit. Did it have to do with Vets?

Old Crow explained the dilemma, the Memorial
tattered by the angry Chief's warriors who
wrecked the day with virulent venom. And now

no movement existed to repair and rebuild
all that had stood true for Natives' stout
men of war. The Bandit nodded and seemed

serious; the details of the damage
made him quite furious. *For sure, I will*
haunt the halls of the Congress

and make those old men finally confess
to their sins of inert uselessness. Let's
form a committee and get them to redress

this. Crow couldn't have been happier, his
face full of dimples. If another silent moment
would have passed, he might have done

a Green Corn Dance measured in inches
then miles. I turned to Crow again and said,
But he's dead. Crow laughed. *But see how*

the dead can kick the living in the head.
We win!
It's like I said.

Jobe and the Middens

> *--In which Burt Reynolds (Bandit) takes us to the Jupiter*
> *Inlet's Jobe Indian mounds, much is revealed about the Ais,*
> *Jaega, and Seminole tribes, Old Crow victoriously exhumes*
> *the buckskin stickball game-ball, and the rhythms of the*
> *Green Corn Dance grow stronger and stronger.*

Bandit had one more promise
to keep: *to reveal the ball!* Had
he thrown it in the deep?

We rode the Mustang to Jupiter
Inlet, a spot where the old Jobe
tribe once lived and thrived,

a branch of the Jeaga who camped
just south and an arm of the Ais
who lived just north—more peoples

who paid tribute to the Calusa.
Bandit said he recalled he might
have stashed the ball somewhere

near a Jobe town and the Middens.
I noted that "Jobe and the Middens"
sounded like the name of a band

like *Josie and the Pussy Cats*. Reynolds
raised an eyebrow, but Crow and Antonia
ignored me. *Or a sixties psychedelic pre-*

prog extravaganza act, I said. Is Jobe
where they got the name for the place
just north of Jupiter, Hobe Sound?

I was in a meditative and contemplative
mind as the tires whined beneath the horse's
hooves. *And what about that subtribe, the Boka-*

Ratónees, a small group of natives who made
a midden in the midst of what now's
The Sanctuary enclave of luxury homes?

Did the Spanish think they'd heard their own
language spoken, and came up with "Boca
Raton," the mouth of the rat, a lame little

beast, more nasty than fat, and found near
that inlet in droves? Bandit slapped my
shoulder. *Slow down there, son.*

Let's not get too far ahead of
ourselves. We've got a buckskin
to find, and a Chief sitting with you

who's gotta game to win.
Antonia pulled up to the Jupiter
Lighthouse, a cylinder painted garnet

and black. The waves in the inlet broke
large and loud. The sea breeze whipped
the palm fronds and flowers of the four-

petal pawpaw. The sun glowed hot;
there were no crowds. Jonathan Dickinson
at first found no one when his ship

wrecked offshore in 1696; but the Jobe
quickly appeared, concerned
about the cargo and less about the lives

of the castaways; no matter, they let
Dickinson and family and others
stay for three days—after they convinced

the natives they were actually Spanish
not English. And the group made
a treacherous journey all the way

to St. Augustine. The Jobe made do
with goods from the ship and others
that tumbled ashore in big storms. Good

trade with Calusa and Mayaimi and Ais,
Jaega and Tequesta and small tribes
on shoresides. They preferred their own

clothes of woven palm breechcloths
and skirts made of deerskin and were
happy for meals of blackfin tuna and shark.

And they built their shell middens
as tall as Calusa's but perhaps
not as elaborate as "King Carlos's"

Stababa. *Odd how the lighthouse
is painted garnet,* said Antonia,
as up the sand-covered shell-hill

we tread. *Perhaps not,* said Crow.
*Others came later, after Anglos
had settled and the Spanish had

gone. The mid-1800s were when
Seminoles and early settlers
got along. They cruised

to Jupiter on dugout canoes
on the Indian River and Loxahatchee
lagoons. Trading became common,*

and soon the Seminoles set camp
near Center Street in the tiny
downtown of Jupiter Beach.

The lighthouse keepers were
especially stocked with exchange-
able goods, and the Natives

spent time there whenever
they could. And Black
Seminoles too would frequent

the town, because since this
was after the Treaty of Eufaula
the Blacks could now remain

in the Seminole Nation. Osceola,
you know, had a Black Seminole
wife, and abhorred slavery

and its strife. But he didn't live
to see these halcyon days
of peace in Jupiter before

the Great Civil War broke out
and poisoned the shores.
Bandit cleared his throat as we reached

the top
of the inlet's
tallest, towering mound.

I recall it might have been near
here, but I was a little bit drunk
when I buried it. Bandit mostly

smiled but seemed sheepish too.
Crow didn't look concerned
as we scanned the Atlantic

and stared at the lighthouse piercing
the sky like a giant's ball stick.
This will do the trick, our big

Chief muttered, and pulled the hickory
from out my back pocket and held it
before him as if a strangely shaped

divining rod. Antonia gave him space
and walked down the slope, and Bandit
and I edged to the rim of the midden.

Old Crow shuffled and mumbled as if
performing his own personal Green
Corn Dance, and then he stood rigid

and at moments adjusted his stance.
A trio of dragonflies swarmed
the stick's tip and a flock of seagulls

cried in the distance. The hickory
dropped slightly, and then Crow let
it touch ground. His fingers gently

rummaged through things in the mound,
broken arrowheads, animal bones,
oyster exteriors, husks of clam shells,

broken pottery shards, perforated
bear teeth, and human metatarsals.
Plenty of sand, of course. And he

kept digging until the hole became
a foot deep or more, until he finally
smiled and pulled up something more

than remains from those days
of the Jobe. In his hand he held
fast, the stickball game's precious

ball. He held it up to the sun and
suddenly became tall. He turned
to the south and gave a great shout,

and then he popped
the deerskin straight
in his mouth.

Mound Key

*--Of the return to the abandoned, long-forgotten Stababa,
Crow's revelation of what's at stake regarding his wager
with Buffalo, the arrival of Chief Buffalo for the final
round of the stickball game, the reappearance of the Long-
Ears-of-the Sea, the rhythms and beats of the Green Corn
Dance that swell louder than ever, and the end of all things
intertwined within this Adventure.*

We three rode the Mustang
to Estero and rented a boat
for the trip out to sea;

we arrived at Mound Key
well before Chief Buffalo
who'd been stuck near Tamiami

making his plans with his
Miccosukee clan. Crow knew
Buffalo would sense when

the ball was uncovered, so we
made for the spot for Old Crow's
last stand, the towering remains

of Stababa. And here's
where Crow made clear
the genius of his ancestors.

They built the island we
stood upon, 126 man-
made acres, a series of Calusa-

constructed mounds towering
fifty feet above the sea
at its pinnacles. *He wants*

the secrets from me, said Crow,
the knowledge of how we
conquered all for 2,000 years

without planting a crop or even
a tree. He wants to know how we
made our cypress masks and statues

and homes so impervious to weather.
And how we ruled for so long
on only fishing. Antonia squinted.

You survived without agriculture?
Crow handed me his stick
and glanced at her. *We lived in and by*

and always around the sea, and we
worshiped the waters, and it worshiped
us back. Look around you! He pointed

at valleys and ramps between the tall
mounds, as large as most Incan or Mayan
creations, he moved his hand across

the landscape of wide grooves. *You see*
the canal that runs straight through
the islet, and on either side of the water-

way you see 50-yard pools, one after another,
connected to the canal by man-
sized openings. Now dry lochs, yes, but

for centuries these small bays made
home for the fish to stay so we could
always feast on any old day. We farmed

the fish! And we had our hidden
ways, ways that Buffalo would love
for me to reveal. And like a fool, when

I'd run out of cash to bet on our game, I swore
as collateral Stababa and the knowhow
that allowed us our name—The Fierce

People, strong from our food; we, the giants
of the Everglades-lands. We ruled all
of Florida with our monstrous hands!

Antonia and I stood in open-
mouthed awe, shocked by Old Crow's
ferocious voice and stern jaw.

But your people are gone, she said.
They're gone for me too. So these aquaculture
secrets can't help us in this new era.

Crow took back the stick and waved it
in a blur. *These are our words, they're more*
precious than song; they live deep inside us

making us strong! They're carved to our souls,
as we transform with each dying, flying from
human to panther or shark or black bear, then

to mouse or mullet or tortoise, then to beetle
or minnow or ant. And as we become more scant,
our minds continue to grow from the sharing

of what makes these middens so sacred; it sticks
to our bones and makes and remakes us.
We cannot give freely the keys of our souls.

As when I'd first met him, the ball in his cheek
made him seem full of chaw, but amazingly the
words neither garbled nor stuck in his craw.

She and I stared at the gulf, not making a sound.
The air smelled of cooked fish, but no fires
blazed. The clouds filled the sun and made a humid,

dark shade. We heard a distant motor so turned
to the east to see Chief Buffalo driving a Whaler
he'd leased. He'd land at Stababa in minutes.

We were one with the land, Crow began, then
cleared his throat. *When the sea level dropped*
in 1250, we crafted those 50-yard watercourts,

but we kept in balance with the bay. And next
we reworked the middens to put old shells
from below up on top, to make our kingdom

tougher than rock. As we walked on the island,
a drizzle sprang from the sky, a soft rain that cooled
and dampened the noise of Buffalo's engine.

Buffalo beached the boat, leaped
from the bow, and started to sprint. He gripped
his ball stick in his powerful hands.

Crow now regained his mojo. He carried
the hickory under one arm and charged
down a shell-ramp and down to

the sand. He ran toward the sandflats low
tide had uncovered. Buffalo, too, fresh off his
boat, made for this muck, an opportune place

to try out their luck. Heat flashes stalked the clouds.
The air, though rain-cold, felt muggy, smelt moldy.
Antonia and I stumbled down from the mound.

When the distance between them became 100
yards, the two chiefs stopped running and glared
at each other from this comfortable distance.
Old Crow, the unacknowledged great, great
grandnephew of Chief Osceola,
nicknamed John Jumper or Cowkeeper
or Billy-Panther, depending on weather,
but named at birth *Ochafanwaw*,
Native American blackbird king!
And Buffalo, the Miccosukee Chief
Buffalo Tiger, Jr., also known
as Heenehatche Jr., was set to swat
at Crow Billy-Panther Ochafanwaw
and break the chief in two.

As we remained stuck in time
not-time, the sea level fell
as it did in 1250, seemingly sucked

down a sink hole, and though we
stood in the present, the past
returned with a vengeance,
changing the landscape.

The Whaler was grounded as the ocean
withdrew. A quarter mile
from the shore of the Key the sea bottom
was dry, all the way to the edge
of a channel. A cement piling stretched
from the muck with a red triangle
on either side and the number 3
prominent on both of its surfaces.

Did Crow and Buffalo not see it?
Here stood not a channel marker
but a single goalpost,
tall, with the triangular-shape
of a Christmas tree. More like
a tree with a very long trunk.
And in the misty drizzle,
I thought I saw atop the post
snail shells and a nest,
and in the nest
a great bald eagle.

Antonia and I jogged toward
the sandbar that the two chiefs
had already reached. They stood
ten feet apart, facing each other
on the beach. Rain grew heavier.

And it appeared as though both men
had pulled a mask from their pants,

masks that were the craft of Calusa—
Had Crow given one to Buffalo?

Each mask had the off-centered
eyes and shape of a shaman-face.

One dried-blood red and the other
more yarrow-yellow. These masked men

danced around each other, waving their
sticks. Did the ball in Crow's cheek

begin to swell? Antonia and I were
walking now, too tired to run.

The pair held their stickball
sticks above their heads, and the sky

thundered and thundered again. And then,
twins! Each hickory branch had divided

in two, and each chief held a stick
in each hand, now the Seminole

ballgame tradition was clearly at hand.
A wind swept down from the top

of the tallest Stababa mound and lifted
Crow off his feet, and for a moment

he flew, but the gale swept
through him and blew the ball

from his mouth, sent it skyward
and a bit to the south. The game had

begun! Down, down, down
dropped the deerskin. Buffalo

slammed into Crow, and the two
wrestled for position beneath

the diving, leather meteor. Their
jousting sticks knocked

each other's masks, and the face-
pieces flew to the sand, and for

a brief moment when their faces
reappeared, their features were

exactly the same, neither Crow
nor Buffalo but possibly

Chief Caalus, a regal nose
on a wide, proud face.

But the rain stopped,
and they then looked themselves.

The ball grew close, and Buffalo
shoved an elbow into Crow's

chest, and Crow stumbled, and
the buckskin landed on

the Miccosukee's stick. The Calusa
up against him, moved a shoulder

to his opponent's chin and their
sticks hit and hit and hit with a

click, click, click! A sound like
branches breaking in a cyclone's

rumble. Buffalo jumped back
two yards or so away as his foe

lost balance, and the man launched
the ball from his stick. It soared

towards the pole. Crow backed
fast to the piling, popped his spine

to the surface and raised both
his hickories straight above

his head, the sticks nearly
becoming one and the same.

He attempted a block, so he would
not lose the game. The shot flew

true but hit against both Crow's
wrists and flew back to Buffalo

and landed back on his stick,
and he stood closer now, only

two feet away, but Crow knew
what he had to do—he dove

into the chief's waist and plowed
him down to the ground. And

the deerskin sprang loose
and rolled across the sand.

Was the tide coming in,
as fast as it had fallen?

Suddenly water lapped
at their feet. They scrambled

for the prize, eyes desperate
and wide, shoulder to shoulder,

sticks spread from their sides,
but Crow's left foot must have hit

a wet spot because his leg plunged
deep, which meant he was caught.

Buffalo scooped up the sphere
and whipped around so fast

because he did not notice Crow
stuck in the sand, and Buffalo sent

the ball arcing high but direct
to the top of the pole and the

eagle's huge nest. The ball
rainbowed deep into sky

and became small
and then large

as if it might blot the sun
and recreate the blue, but

just then a big darkness
fell over the scene

as if a monster-diamond
of night had arisen, a twist

in a dream. Antonia grew
slack-jawed; I dropped, shocked,

to my knees. The chiefs
just stared, seeming unpleased—

or was it disbelief? For out
of the sea had jumped

that unfettered beast,
the Long-Ears-of-the-Sea,

We-waw Hycko Capko, the dire
wolf like a manta, the devil-ray,

the Sea-Wolf that preys
in these waters.

And so its mouth did open,
as if a lidless box,

and there did the ball
now finally drop.

The beast crashed downwards,
slapped the sea like a god-hand,

soaked us completely, and washed
the chiefs further backwards. Then

Long Ears quickly vanished, swimming
down to the deep. A ball in its belly.

How long would it keep?

Antonia leaned over to me
and whispered a question,
*Did you see that moment
when they became twins?*
I stood and nodded.
She pursed her lips.
*Are those two the true doubles
in all this and their infinitely
expansive and endless game?*
I didn't know; instead, I said,
*Maybe it's as simple as
your twin is your best friend
who always lives inside you.*

Buffalo, now over his shock,
like a rocket darted into
the gulf, swimming like
a madman for the Long Ears
with the deerskin. He swam
and swam and soon swam
out of sight. Crow laughed
long and louder than we'd
ever heard him before. He
danced in our direction and
handed me his hickory—
it'd become one stick again—
and said, *This is yours. Keep
it safe. If Buffalo can catch
the manta, then you will be
my caddy again.* I bowed and held
it tightly in my palm and imagined
it a wand-of-plenty to remake
myself with future plans. *But
you will need it, won't you,
if I'm not around?* I asked.
*Well, I can always
make another, or have one
made for me. But it takes
a long time to catch a Sea-
Wolf once it heads out
to deeper waters. My secrets
are safe for now. For now,
I will return to work
on the Niña, Pinta, and
Santa María.* He laughed
again; his smile was broad.

Antonia and I rode the Mustang
to *la casa de su abuela* in Orlando.
We raced along the interstates,
the windows open, the noise loud.
All this doubling and doubling
finally had ceased. Only silence echoed
across the waters. The air's trembling
stopped, all molecules in time and space
cleanly separated between two sorts
of the same universe; the dreams had paused
to await a new cycle. Antonia would
soon return to Cuba to seek
others who might have Calusa
blood, to find her twins-of-heart,
those whose pupils, in their eyes,
as Calusa believed, contained their
main soul. I, on the other hand,
would aim for Seminole, the county,
where Apopka waited, its ungainly
youth center filled with children
who'd maybe stare in awe
at the stick of *Ochafanwaw*
that I'd show them on the first
day, before our recess started,
and all came out to play.

Michael Trammell lives in the Florida panhandle. He's published a novel, *Rad Sick Record*, a poetry collection, *Our Keen Blue House*, and a textbook, *Business Communication Everywhere*. Other work has appeared in *New Letters, Sandhill Review, Florida Flash, The Chattahoochee Review, Pleiades, SoFloPoJo*, and *G.W. Review*. He's a Senior Lecturer at Florida State University, where he teaches technical writing and professional speaking, and an associate editor for the *Apalachee Review*. In the summers he frequently works abroad in either London, Florence, or Valencia, Spain.

Hysterical Books
2026